Concerning
the Holy Ghost's
Interpretation of
J. Crew Catalogues

Concerning the Holy Ghost's Interpretation of J. Crew Catalogues

Elizabeth A.I. Powell

LEAKY BOOT PRESS

Concerning the Holy Ghost's Interpretation of
J. Crew Catalogues
by Elizabeth A.I. Powell

Acknowledgements

'Spring/Summer Catalogue, 1998'
originally appeared in
Black Warrior Review

First published in 2019
by Leaky Boot Press

ISBN: 978-1-909849-65-5

In memory of
Don Itkin

Prologue

That whosoever looks at a catalogue shall see himself as he should like to be, not as he truly is.

That, though the photograph shows him a picture of a mountain climber in a purple mountain climber's suit, and the viewer of the catalogue photograph believes inside his heart he is as a mountain climber is, he is really not a mountain climber.

That, because real truth is obscured by the images of our earthly delight, we shall only see ourselves as unattainable things dancing around the impenetrable circle of what we'd like to be.

That, until we can see clearly the way of the flower to the sun, we shall dwell in the photograph of the free world, forever and ever. Amen.

—the Holy Ghost moves words in the copywriter's dream as he sleeps in his room of burgundy velvet on the East Side of New York City.

I

Spring/Summer Catalogue
1998

Even though Wolfgang Ackerbloom changed the lens on his Leica twice, the ocean remained blue. He could still faintly see the freckles on Mindy's nose. And Helene, the one in the passenger seat, the one with long brown hair pushed behind her ears? She seemed to be gloriously inhaling something from last night's dreams. Absolutely, she was smelling the scent iced tea makes when the ice cubes crack in a large crystal clear tumbler, lemons floating aimlessly about.

Here at the scene of page twelve, Wolfgang could smell the fishy scent of life revealing itself, hear the waves lapping upon the rocks. Mostly, Wolfgang and his large, virile nose could smell anything, even shit from four miles away. Predatorily, he prided himself on this. When he looked out from behind the body of his camera, he saw the water as cornflower blue. To him, it was the longing of a jazz song. The warm beckoning sand, Atlantic beige. It was the color of a comfortable, clean kitchen in winter, the Xs on the days of December, silk sweater number A35 on page 117. Wolfgang set up his equipment. He was late now, everyone was waiting.

Mindy sat in the 1964 sea blue Cadillac out of her mind on diet pills, pretending to be driving to the other side of the beach where the male models from page 42 were doing handstands in the sand. Pasteled, heathered, sleeveless, the dress she wore was an India plaid. Like a dream of white skin and reflecting sun, Helene moved in and out of the car, waiting and moving.

"Yeah, but," Wolfgang wanted to know from his skinny, pale, long-legged assistant who was twenty-five and freshly-shaven, "does it look like 1964, 1964 lost and regained?"

Almost smirking, the assistant shrugged his left shoulder. He wasn't even born yet in 1964. Neither was Mindy who, as she sat in the stationary Cadillac on the beach, began conjuring up in her mind the past she had not lived. Rows of old-fashioned hair dryers in a pink beauty parlor, the smell of waxed floors, black and white photographs of men in thin black ties leaning back toward walls at cocktail parties, the fixed dizziness of first nursery memories—this was what Mindy saw when she thought of 1964, though she wouldn't even be born for another four years. In her mind she saw her parents in their own private rendition of *Barefoot in the Park*. This was not what Wolfgang wanted. He was alive in 1964. Penny loafers, steamer trunks for college, brown electric blankets, impending change, that was what Wolfgang thought represented the era he was searching for in the photograph.

"I don't know what 1964 looks like," Wolfgang's assistant told him, "but I think it smells like Niagara Spray and Starch."

That's it. 1964 was clean. Look clean, Wolfgang thought. Clean and easy. Clean sea blue Cadillac, pretend the ocean is clean. Mindy and Helene were declared virgins by Wolfgang's photographic imagination. "For Christ's sake," Wolfgang directed, "put a cashmere sweater over the seat of the car."

Helene and Mindy smiled and didn't smile, tilted and didn't tilt, swayed and didn't sway. The fury of the moment was a pulse that sounded like *act of god, act of god, act of god*. It was this energy that caused Mindy some anxiety. Helene believed it was because someone had been dreaming of love.

But then Wolfgang shouted "That's what it looks like! What does it feel like?" The assistant was getting a headache, felt as if he were playing twenty questions with his Alzheimer's grandfather. He couldn't smell the shit Wolfgang smelled, but that was what made Wolfgang so great.

When Wolfgang shouted, "Jesus Christ! Make it feel like 1964," he was appealing to the realm of the irretrievable, he was really asking for a second chance at desire. The images Wolfgang wanted for the layout spoke to sustaining in the present what no longer was, and making that the elixir for being in the unfathomable moment. Wolfgang wanted the mystery of why 1964 no longer existed shown to him, and this was another aspect of his desire for life. For somewhere in him, he knew that to recapture the image of the past in the present was the nectar of the gods, the taste of no longer needing the mystery of desire and time, but living simultaneously in and about it without fear or regret or necessity. When he shouted out like he did, small beads of sweat gathering just under his hairline, he was, almost, asking for the world to stop.

In the Cadillac the cigarette lighter had been pushed in and forgotten. It no longer remembered to push itself out when it was burning. Inside its little tunnel the edge of the cigarette lighter was hot, its round coils a bright, apocalyptic red. The buttons on the radio were just that: buttons to push, and they were an aqua enamel. There was only AM. In the back seat of the car was a boom box that you couldn't see in the picture. It was where the Supreme's tape was playing, *Baby Love, Oh Baby Love...* In the trunk, there were three hunter green beach chairs made out of nylon and cotton. They were there until they were to be delivered onto another photo shoot, where Wolfgang would pose the models around these chairs on the front lawn of an easy, white summer cape, where long beach grasses took over the side of the house. In the glove compartment, the car's crumpled papers from the eighty-year old restaurateur and Jewish Mafioso from Brooklyn sat with a thickening smell of mildew. The man who owned this car loved beautiful women and his nephew worked in the design department, which rented this car for the shoot.

There was no dust in the car, and the two young women, Mindy and Helene, felt very comfortable in the seats. The day was not too hot so no one's limbs stuck to the mock leather. Always in the distant backs of Mindy's and Helene's ears, they could hear Wolfgang saying "More Cape Codish. More 1964."

"I know he just wants to get down your pants," Helene whispered to Mindy.

"That's all these photographers want," she added, trying to be sisterly, but Mindy found it insulting. Wolfgang was twice, maybe three times, Mindy's age. Helene knew what to say to Mindy, beyond what she has said, but never said it. Almost seven years ago now, Helene's father told her not to become a model because she would have to sleep her way to the top. Still this was not the case for her, yet every time she heard Wolfgang speak or move his body she thought of her father's words. When Mindy looked at Wolfgang, his long, graying brown hair, his deep-set green eyes, she thought subconsciously about her father, but in a different way. She swam in the subconscious thought as if she were an orange carnival goldfish in a tank full of fuchsia, cobalt blue, and lime green pebbles. How wonderful it was to swim inside the small tank of her psyche, her life. Mindy believed Wolfgang was a mythic creature, a satyr with a lens, sent to document her as the ancients had documented their stories, their muses. She loved his shape, his heft, and seductive lack of grace. His was the Romanesque nose of someone who knew how to unchain her refrigerator of a heart.

As Helene and Mindy pretended to ride slowly by the ocean, cat-shaped tortoiseshell sunglasses and cotton scarves of blue and red on their heads, there was a grace that told a story underneath the appearance of the photo shoot. The two women pretended to make their way toward a magical beach hut on a sandy shore of a solicitous paradise. Wolfgang shot rapidly, he was undertaking the action of artistic license, trying to get the models to evoke something, and by doing so he opened himself up to what resided deep within him. Every image, every dream.

He considered the aspects of composition. The way the sea blue Cadillac sat upon the asphalt that came right up to the sand. The pine trees off to the right in the distance. Helene and Mindy's pastel-colored plaid summer dresses, the scarves on their heads. There was a pitcher of iced tea on a gingham-covered table that was not in the shoot. There was the smell of the warm tea breaking the ice cubes that no one could see. And then there were the freckles on Mindy's nose ripening in the midday sun. As he zoomed in on her face, Wolfgang considered how Helene's smile was the smile of delicate cover-up, protection from other people's dreams. But it was Mindy's face that held him in the cradle of his longing. For in the sea blue 1964 Cadillac, Mindy Abbot was free.

When, after the layout was shot, the catalogue printed and mailed out, a middle-aged blonde woman named Kyra Snelling, a Senator's wife, waited for something to happen as she sat drinking cappuccino on her deck that overlooked the ocean in Westport, Connecticut. There, this woman studied the catalogue, envious of what the catalogue somehow seemed to represent. She admired Mindy's look of wistful agility on page twelve, and in this she saw herself lost in California, a French knot in her hair, people in hats, music she couldn't hear but feel, the sun hitting her face at right angles. The sun was hitting her face in a way that she could only feel in her imagination. This was what constituted her longing, and it had to do with how she imagined herself in the sun and faraway. It had to do with the fact that she had grown into this particular woman looking at catalogues, not the one she thought she would become.

And it was this woman, who could see the ocean not very far at all from her Westport home, who looked instead at the catalogue, staring at Mindy and Helene as they drove by the ocean in their beautiful clothes toward an unknown destination. This woman was moved and thus decided to buy the plaid dress for eighty-eight dollars, because somehow the picture reminded her of the time before she married, when she used to ride innocently around with her girlfriends smoking menthol cigarettes somewhere in time circa 1964. In her state of remembering, she bought the dress, even though she had one very similar to it which she could wear if she were not always so engrossed in the mail order catalogues she received. The picture of Mindy reminded her that she has grown to know too much about the world. Lunch dates, a happy discontentment, and KY Jelly have become her captors.

For blessed were Mindy's diet pills, for they helped to make her free. Blessed are too many diet pills when Mindy stood alone in memory; she therefore blacked out. But here captured on page twelve of the catalogue was the moment when Mindy was at the height of her speeded frenzy, meeting each click of the camera, each click of the speed in her brain with a facial expression so pure, so true, she sold a quarter-million of these dresses.

But this is what the photo could not tell us. For in order to evoke the feeling of 1964, Mindy imagined that she was her mother. She was her mother driving her father's 1964 sea blue Cadillac on the road next to the water from Greenwich, Connecticut to New York City where she would meet Rabbi Mendelson of the Reform Beth Israel Temple. Happily, oh so happily, Mindy drove and drove, pretending to drive, pretending to be her mother. Her mother in a pretty pastel-colored plaid dress, so in love and ready to convert for the sake of her husband-to-be. Wolfgang fired away with his camera until it clicked and jarred open 1964. The camera like the wind pushing spirit around, capturing it and moving it. Wolfgang bent at the knees, moved closer, bent at the waist. All the while he said more, yes, more and Mindy fell more deeply into her mother's memory, which had been trailing her like stars.

Imagining, slightly haphazard, Mindy turned deeper into the chameleon of her mother. Pretending to accelerate into 1965, she believed she would change everything about herself. As her mother, she drove the sea blue Cadillac toward New York City, far away from the quietly crucifixed Oneida county town to marry the Jewish man she met at State University. She would move to Brooklyn Heights, give dinner parties, learn how to make chopped liver, tell a Jewish joke. She would pancake herself in an effort to rid herself of freckles, remorse, resolve, and resurrection. Methodically, she would learn how to put her face down slowly in her bathwater, blowing bubbles from her nose in the hot water, and thus expunge the last drop of her past into the good waters of New York City. She would scrub and banish away the green mosquito nights, the scouring, penitent barn days. At high speeds, she would drive straight through the stupefying, humiliating silence of her youth, the tragedy and disgust of her parentage, straight into 1968 where she would conceive Mindy while she was drunk on Seder wine, and then try to make her everything she tried to be but couldn't.

As she looked at the waves crest and fall from the corner of her eye, feeling the light cast shadows on the breast that contained her febrile, ambiguous, yet amenable heart, Helene hoped that whatever it was that Mindy was working herself up into had nothing to do with the dreams anyone was having. Incessantly and avidly, Helene believed that the dreams of others helped mold her life, lives in general, any life. She could not look back to 1964 because she felt she didn't know what people dreamt about then. This was what she would always know—that whatever Mindy was thinking, she was not thinking clearly, and that to sleep with Wolfgang Ackerbloom was to make the big, irreversible mistake.

The two women continued their body motions, their posing while a large fan went round and around in it's cage. Mindy began to slip into conjugal fantasies of Wolfgang by virtue of the smell he imposed like a tiger's cage around her. It was a smell that captivated Mindy in a way she was not fully aware of, leading her through the jungle of her own memory and desire. Helene thought only of the fact that the false wind felt burdensome on her face, as burdensome as the future would be to Mindy one day. Mindy looked briefly into Helene's eyes, and felt as if she couldn't focus, as if she had tapped into some fear, some anxiety that resided in Helene that she couldn't wholly see herself. She wanted to ask Helene questions, but didn't know where to begin.

During these moments, a white-haired copywriter in New York City was falling asleep on his purple office sofa, dreaming of the Helene he had seen on his desk in photographs, a sweet, decent Helene wrapped in the gossamer of mysterious things, the sun-ripened cotton durability and rayon softness of sanctification, acceptance, and silk-lined love. In the car, somehow eased, Helene smiled at Mindy, laughed, reached out and grabbed her hand, raising their linked arms toward the sun. Life seemed so strange. Mindy began to laugh. And the ocean remained cornflower blue, the sand Atlantic beige. Poplin, seersucker, straw hat, cotton roll-neck. High gloss, percentages, metaphors for living.

Wolfgang shot it all. Finally, he smelled it, he got it right. And in the photo that made it to page twelve, we see the two women stopped in the very moment when they each considered in their own way that everything they did from that moment on would change their lives irrevocably. India plaid, the pink-clouded ocean sky, just for that moment, before it passed into nothingness, they were lacking nothing and everything.

And the copywriter continued to dream purely of Helene.

Intermezzo

2.44 a.m., GMT
En Route to the Taj Mahal, in Flight From the
East Side of New York City, Lament 1

(… My world is a shattered mirror. Glistening, disjointed, this is what is incomprehensible: that everything is God. Oh, to be spirit tangled in this web of image, the feelings of seeing. For earth's images are my wings, terrible movement that I've become.

Yet there is something I can never forget even though I am responsible, even though I know the answer: why was there a forbidden fruit in paradise? I will always ask: was it even necessary? And out of so many possibilities why was nakedness part of the outcome? That in the end it comes down to the realization of images? And what is my part in this? It's this constant agitation…)

II

Summer Catalogue
1998

On the enclosed porch of an old white cape, Wolfgang's assistant set down and then spun an antique beige and brown globe that depicted a world that no longer existed. As the globe spun and settled, the porch continued to smell of old books, with wafts of salty sea breeze and honeysuckle from the trellis floating by on the tepid air. The long stalks of grass by the side of the house wavered in the wind. A shoeless boy with sand between his toes stood in his yard next door and listened to the perplexing sound of crickets.

Authoritatively, Wolfgang loaded his camera. His assistant adjusted the lights. Wolfgang needed a soft light for poplin, seersucker, and twill. When he looked up from his camera, he scanned around for Helene. He felt somehow haunted by a presence of her. He felt as if she was onto something he couldn't recognize, and that this was somehow detrimental to him. He fully realized he could not smell the gardenia perfume scent of Mindy that Helene had complemented earlier. When Wolfgang sensed Helene smelling, and talking of the fragrance of Mindy, he returned back to the lavender scent of his mother's love of women.

Just barely, Mindy knew Wolfgang was growing tired of her. When she sat across from him during breaks, when she looked into the green pulpit of his eyes, all she could see in her mind's eye was the dull, deadening glaze of her stepmother's jade ring. Each time she felt him pull away from her, walking different routes around the white cape of a house, the way his eyes glared, Mindy felt that she was inhaling thousands of jade rings that sat like tacks in the lining of her throat. She moved toward Wolfgang to relieve this feeling. Almost medically, medicinally, she felt the heat and musk of his body, a soothing expectorant, a temporary sedative against a series of actions that set the jade ring of her stepmother into a tiring, debilitating motion. But she needed him, and each time they climbed upon each other's naked bodies and into the obscured and almost forgotten corners of night, she felt a distance between them, a distance created out of jade and musk and lavender, it was breathing and being and waking. It was a distance that contained their own private temple of worship.

For Wolfgang, each time they made love, he couldn't bear the fragility of Mindy's bones beneath him. It made him feel as if he were heavy as stone, so he moved her on top of him, so he could see her face unobstructed by bed covers and his long hair. Each time he couldn't help but smell his own past in his desire, the scent of old gardening books where a single violet from his mother's lover has been pressed against words like graft and cuttings.

So when Mindy came onto the set of the enclosed porch, Wolfgang avoided the glances of what he believed to be her cruel rain eyes. They seemed to him torrential, bearing storm. Waiting for the shoot to begin, Helene circled the house, waiting and walking and feeling the movements of dreaming humming about her like honeybees. Alert, yet in a world shaded by the hues of her own beliefs, she felt certain she was onto someone dreaming of her again. She rounded the house, again and again. Then she moved inside the house, and rounded the central wall that divided the foyer from the kitchen. As she paced inside waiting for make-up, she saw a white lily in her mind's eye. This meant, to her, that she was suddenly remembering walking up a paved suburban road in New York, houses on each side, until there was a long patch of grass made up of weeds and no one's grass, and a monarch butterfly smashed into her skirted thigh. The sun shined and there; to her left, in the long neglected grass, grew a single hybrid white lily. Then there came the urgency of the helicopter that flew above her in this memory. This was the image that she paced on, waiting to confront whatever it was that was disturbing her tranquility, moving her back and forth through odd points in her memory. She knew that whatever dream was seeping into her life, it had the urgent sound of that helicopter, it had the holiness of the white lily, the daring of the monarch butterfly, the dour sensibility of suburban grids. She wondered when and if, in her life, this existence among so many images and feelings would ever bear a fruit she could eat, a fruit that would satiate and fill and answer.

Thus began the Summer 1998 catalogue shoot. Each person's memories and musings bounced off the others, creating clatter in everyone's mind. Wolfgang had two sticks of black licorice hanging from his mouth, and though he thought he knew who he was, he did not. Really, he was eating a prop, the licorice from the menswear sequence. Like the predatory cat of sleeping kingdoms, Helene could smell the licorice from her fold-up wooden chair. She was having a final touch of bronze-colored powder put above her bosom. Wolfgang had decided that the green lawn chairs from the trunk of the sea blue Cadillac would not do at all for any aspect of the shoot around this house. Instead, an old white-painted iron bed had been moved in to the corner of the screened-in porch.

Gracefully, Helene moved barefoot across the gray-painted floor. "Come here," Wolfgang said to her and pointed to the bed. Helene saw him as a ray of light that had taken her by surprise. It seemed something was in the process of changing within him. Mindy was lying on the old metal bed, on top of cream-colored bedspreads. She was wearing a pinstriped oxford men's shirt in blue and white. The cotton on the bed was soft. The male models from page forty-two were playing a trumpet off in the backyard of the house where the stylist had set up laundry hanging, and had agonized over which underwear, which socks, which vintage house-dresses to put on the old rope line. Mindy looked at Wolfgang and smiled. Inside the porch of the easy white cape, Wolfgang's assistant adjusted the lights yet again, and sunlight came in through the honeysuckled trellis and onto the bed. It made the shapes of shadow puppets and shamrocks over Mindy's body. Underneath her extra rib, Mindy felt the place that the light could not touch, not because there was impenetrable sadness there, but because it was a place that moved the feelings of memory through her body. It was tender, like lips that would kiss, mixed with the solitude of the ancillary place, so un-seeable, so harshly felt. Each time Mindy felt the soft cotton against her feet and legs, this spot in her body felt like a white peony opening against the rainy morning memory of a long ago June stored in the black and white window of her mind. To her the peony represented a self-longing for the pure self that would never completely open. Indeed, she knew herself enough, in a desperate sort of way, and felt the hunger of that incomplete knowledge. She sensed the blue of her irises reflecting the dance of the trellis light, that the light that entered her eyes could be candles burning too brightly in a winter kitchen where apples were being baked. She felt Wolfgang's winter spreading over her, like the smell of his body. As she lied on the bed, she wanted to close her eyes, and imagine Wolfgang's hand running up her side. The thought made her stretch her legs, arch her back. Wolfgang's lens got in close to her body for a tight shot of her face and shirt. Mindy could smell the summer grass, and the newly washed bed linen, which had been hung out in the sun. She was trying her best to enter Wolfgang's winter, but Helene got on the bed with her.

"I'm after the appearance of two famous women taking a break during a Cape Cod artists' retreat," Wolfgang called out to the set. A teenage boy wearing a cut-up flannel shirt carried a small armload of mildewed books with handsome bindings, and put them on the small pine work desk that sat next to the bed. Everything Wolfgang instructed these people to do was an attempt to recall something that was not wholly there, or theirs.

"Today," Wolfgang said "we are thinking circa 1940. Today we are thinking about what we are." Helene looked down at her cleavage popping out over a navy blue bikini top. Mindy moved, lying diagonally across the bed on her stomach, her feet dangled over the edge, her elbows bent and propping. Pretending to read one of the mildewed books, she suddenly felt suffocated by Helene's skin so close to her. The artificial light began to make Mindy feel nervous, reminding her of the way a refrigerator lights into the dark of night, exposing emptiness and a sort of dreariness. But, now she sighed, for she tried desperately to think as a great young woman artist enjoying herself on a bed some Sunday fifty years ago, but with more revealing clothes on.

Wolfgang began listing famous women artists out loud as he pivoted around the bed. He told Helene to stand up and then fall down on her knees. Mindy grabbed a pillow. Someone came over with hair and make-up brushes and stood by. Trying to act a part, trying to get Wolfgang to come closer with his dreams and his camera so that she could shatter them, Helene thought of what Eudora Welty might do if she were sitting on an old bed on a Cape Cod porch with Katherine Anne Porter. Really, she thought Wolfgang's idea was stupid because it was based on the belief that what was past was somehow richer than what existed right now, how he couldn't see that the past was woven into each thing in the present, that he didn't have to try to hold time like a colicky baby. But she played Wolfgang's game, smiling and tilting, moving, intending, and fell into it like a child into mud. She was, after all, a professional. These days were physically grueling and she avoided any drug that promised to relieve the exhaustion, both physical and mental, no matter what some doctors told her.

Wolfgang said, "Say something to each other." Helene considered very briefly; she remembered the book she got for Christmas from her brother, photographs taken by Welty. Really, she knew nothing of Eudora Welty, except what she had learned at Waldorf High School as a teenager, that Welty wrote short stories and took pictures. She was the only great woman artist Helene could think of who might have been alive during the time Wolfgang was talking about. Helene liked Welty's photographs, felt they showed how dreams hovered over places, exposed wrinkles, desperation, and lust. Plus, Helene believed there was something to the air in Mississippi, a heaviness that was akin to an illuminating, palpable, biblical sadness.

"Probably," she told Mindy, "I would take your photograph now." Helene looked at Mindy's nose, how it was thin and slightly elongated at the end, how the kerchief on top of her head hid her golden, pear-colored hair. Thinking about what Wolfgang said he wanted in this shot, Helene surmised that if she were Eudora Welty, the air would smell like Indian spice, like Lucky Tiger after-shave in a Mississippi barbershop in May after a mild, but lonely winter. She believed that if Wolfgang's photo was to be what he wanted, the image he sought, she should imagine that beneath her lips she hid a fabulously understated gap between her two front teeth. She imagined a thick glass filled with lemonade, condensation running down the sides, a Mississippi Fourth of July. She knew she must imagine herself in tan-colored, silk stocking held up by old garters, inside herself a dark mood hiding. Above all, she knew that if she could not see Mindy as the image of a young Katherine Anne Porter, she must see her as a woman who had recently been graduated from college, and spent the summer reading Anna Karenina on the coast of Spain before she came here to lie on this white iron bed. She knew she must feel that tie between women friends, the innocent wanting of reassurances, the gentle touching and fixing of hair, the wonderment and glad distance of being so close only by words. Assuredly, she knew she must want to photograph Mindy, and find in her a road back to her own self.

But Helene's quiet honesty frightened Mindy. Wolfgang was the gate that held back everything she didn't understand. That was why Mindy wanted to be with Wolfgang. He was her amulet. She tried to keep thinking of loving Wolfgang, and whenever she did she smelled snow freshly fallen. She did not want Wolfgang to expect her to be Helene's Katherine Anne Porter or girl in Spain. Helene looked Mindy right in the eye. Wolfgang held his Leica in his left hand. He wanted everything to be a testimony to what he saw as the evaporation of things that tried to hold onto the nucleus of now.

But, really, the image he was after for this shoot was one of winter waiting to get hold of the fleetingness of summer. Taking the swizzler of licorice out of his mouth with his right hand, he decided that if he had anything to do with it, he would shoot the next summer catalogue in the snow and to hell with what anyone said. He yearned for the intimacy of winter. Mindy couldn't tell if her longing was from being on the bed with Helene, from wanting Wolfgang, or from being caught in between the silent intentions of things.

Wolfgang noticed this. Finally, he thought, he was getting what he wanted. He wanted to expose Mindy and Helene down to their coldest bones and turn them into divine apparitions. He wanted to show the nectar of the world he was born into. He wanted more depth; he wanted an x-ray of his whole life, but he had to use color film. This was the world, he thought to himself, where everything lived in simultaneity. And then a headache. Seeing the two women lying on the bed, he remembered walking in on his mother lying on top of another woman, and now all Wolfgang could smell was the lavender smell of his mother. With the camera in his face, he had a thousand eyes.

Mindy sensed that Wolfgang felt uneasy. To her, he looked slightly faint and aggravated, although all he was doing was holding his camera and squinting at the iron bed from over where he stood by the screen. The way he bent his knees and then straightened them made him look like an ungraceful dancer. Watching him, Mindy felt she had no sense of a woman's greatness beyond what she felt in her own body. She was building dreams, to hell with what Wolfgang wanted or didn't want.

As Mindy's glance moved off into the day that lay beyond the white cape, Wolfgang tried to flee by entering into what he believed was Mindy's daydream. Though he could not truly access it, the belief and feeling of entering Mindy's reverie as if entering a room gave him space within himself to concentrate. He shot and he shot. He sweated. He found refuge in Mindy; he found fear in her, too. Honeysuckle filled the air. In his concentration on Mindy and Helene, his exposing and knowing of them and the clothes that they wore and the faces they made, images of a cabin in winter came intermittently to Wolfgang. So, in a sense, he entered Mindy's daydream where she walked through snowdrifts toward him. In her mind she was wearing snowshoes and she could see how his green eyes were a close relative to the icicles that reflected the pine trees that lined the road of their winter daydream where it was nearing dusk, and from the path to the cabin they could see a small light coming from the kitchen window. Then they were standing at the door to the cabin. Mindy was pushing the door open with her left hip, feeling her body weight move across space, assuring herself that she was still, in fact, a body in motion. Wolfgang, she imagined, was savoring this moment just as she was, the anticipation of the warmth of the cabin, the soft bed that waited for them. Though Mindy's dream did not account for it, in this scenario there was a certain feeling to the moment, the feeling being that each earlier moment had led up to this moment making it unique, accounting for time.

Outside Mindy's daydream, there was the still presentness of the easy white cape that must imagine itself to be on Cape Cod. Wolfgang, of course, did not demand anything of the house itself, except that it be willing to be exposed, be willing to become a part of page twenty-two. Inside it was the comfort of emptiness. There was only a rug filled with hues of gold. The design in it made small and large pyramids alongside crosses and stars and outlines of birds. Upstairs all of the French windows were open, and white Dutch lace curtains fluttered in the breeze, hiding the nakedness of each bedroom. All of the walls were the color of the apricots that sat in a woven tin fruit stand in the sun on page eighty-seven, by the drying laundry in the backyard of the easy white cape. Concerning the color of the apricots, the word Turkish came to Wolfgang. Each window was a reflection of a wash of green and beige from outside. Inside was the climbing scent of the honeysuckle. The naked floors were joyously bare, clean to behold. The paint had been stripped away leaving the exposed pine, which has been rubbed with oil.

Out on the porch, on the bed, imagining Mississippi, imagining whom she and Mindy could be, or really are, Helene felt as if the blue sky was opening out from the center of her stomach, from the place where sensory memory beckoned and twinged. She could suddenly taste lunch counter grits, she felt the sun turning her hair a reddish tinge. Each simple thought was delightful to her. But only the thought was delightful; to actually be there would not have had the same effect, for Helene would then be a different person, not the one of her desirous imagination. She reached out to touch Mindy on the arm.

Looking at this drove Wolfgang toward a greater anguish. He had not expected this feeling. Mindy struggled to meet him in her daydream as if she were a mother comforting a child. Wolfgang's Leica became like an enforcer. But Helene was already penetrated by the lens, and Mindy did not know how to be. As the two women moved about the bed, he thought he saw their individual truths in their eyes, a reflection of a desire he felt they must have for each other. This drove him toward a hard, unclear place within himself. With his camera in hand, Wolfgang confused each closeness and intimacy with the other. Every intimacy Wolfgang thought he witnessed got tangled up in his past. This made the shoot longer than it should have been. Helene suspected this, and began to understand that Wolfgang's thoughts polluted the air like carbon monoxide, contaminating everything with a sort of smog.

Mindy and Helene moved off the bed.

Wolfgang's assistant sealed the rolls of film into a bag. Once the photo that would be used for page twenty-two was developed, printed, retouched, clipped and made ready, the message the white-haired, dreaming copywriter dreamt of would appear as the caption above the page twenty-two photograph of Mindy and Helene—*Tell a Summer Story*.

And in a few months the woman near Westport, Connecticut would pick up her mail, and flip through the catalogue. She'd turn to page twenty-two, and see Mindy and Helene on the white iron bed. She would buy the seersucker blazer and navy blue bikini top that Helene modeled because she believed in the nakedness of love, because, like Helene, she believed there were so many pathways to it. She would buy the oxford shirt Mindy wore, because she had feared love, too. Like Helene she had feared her own nakedness, and embraced it. She would buy these clothes because she was no longer sure what the composition of her self said when she tried reading her face in the car rearview mirror.

But before that, before the copywriter even dreamed his dream, even before Wolfgang handed his assistant the last roll of film, Helene's bikini top, number 3671 in midnight navy, dropped to the floor of the dressing room in the white cape of a house, and she knew deep down that even that day itself had an air of uselessness in the face of time, that what was truly rich were the sun-drenched days spent dwelling in the heart of what makes us who we are not.

Intermezzo

2.43 a.m., GMT
En Route to New York City
from Stonehenge

(… Is not my cardinal law that no one is as they appear to themselves or others? That when the stories of dreams are told in pictures there are no words to express the longing that is sanctified only in the looking, the remembering. I am this remembering, this looking…)

2:42 AM, GMT, New York City. Before departing this is what is observed.

(… watching the sleeping copywriter, his legs tangled in lavender bed linen, while his well-coiffed wife sits at her desk off the kitchen looking over last year's taxes for the audit. She does not feel my presence as she sits figuring, a pencil behind her ear, but she remembers sitting in the car ten years ago, waiting for her husband to come outside with a brick of cheese. Funny, she wonders out of all moments, why she remembers ones like this, ones that seem meaningless… She is hungry.

Inside the bedroom, her husband, the white-haired copywriter sleeps, believing Helene is near. Dreaming, he thinks he whispers lovers' words. He tells her: resurrection cannot be photographed. And then in sleep, he feels as if he is falling, plummeting, tossed by the wind, and in this falling, most of all he is experiencing the feeling of image. And when he awakes the following day, he will not remember the dream, only the falling, only that somehow he has been touched by love, by strange inspiration that takes and receives, that directs and leaves. That, in fact, he does have a whole other life in dreams. It is in his work where he tries to speak to the point of this self-divergence that he feels, and sometimes calls spirituality. Sometimes he thinks he is getting old. These are the words that come to him at the breakfast table, over coffee, over corn flakes, over the *Wall Street Journal*, feeling as though he has touched love.

In the name of
a one hundred and eight dollar seersucker blazer,
the world is made free.
And our dreams? They will continue to be dreams ...)

III

Page 25

Fall/Winter Catalogue
1998

Mindy stood in the kitchen in long underwear. Her hair had been tasseled, her skin powdered and made up so that it was the perfect cream complement to the white union suit she wore. She stood near a small white electric stove. The stylist, in a black pantsuit, brought in a stack of polka-dotted mixing bowls in various shades of blue, and placed them down on the counter next to the stove. Mindy pushed herself up and sat on the counter next to them. Then the stylist brought in handfuls of wooden utensils, which she placed in a large yellow canister. Mindy slides down from the countertop and looked around for the bunch of bananas she saw someone with earlier. She felt hungry. It was early morning. She still had not eaten. Wolfgang looked up at her from his seat where he re-read his notes from the agency.

Back in New York, where Wolfgang wished he was, the well-rested, white-haired copywriter was coming up with a line for the pajama spread—*What Was She Wearing* When? He imagined what the photograph would look like that might accompany his tentative headline. He imagined Helene. He had seen photos of her, in the early summer catalogue, regaling in the open breeze of a sea blue Cadillac as it made its way toward the west, toward a small, straw beach hut. Whenever he looked at her photograph, all he could remember was running through the football field with his brothers in fall during the days of his youth. He remembered how the tulip trees shed in the spring storms by his house. How he had made a small apartment for himself under the house's interior stairs, importing his mother's furniture into his secret dwelling space where he dreamed of women he would someday have and make his own. Now, in the mornings when there were strawberries for breakfast, whenever he put one to the tips of his lips, he always saw Helene in his mind's eye. Then he closed his own hazel-colored eyes and swallowed and was full.

But in the easy summer cape where Wolfgang would have it be winter, Mindy's stomach grumbled. So, Helene gave her half of the last bagel. As Mindy chewed, she saw that Wolfgang and his team had finally gotten the shot set up as they would like it. Wolfgang had finished reading his notes. Mindy saw he had hoarded the deliciously ripe bananas to use in the polka-dotted mixing bowl.

"We're going to do a series of shots in all the different variations of the loungewear," Wolfgang told Mindy and Tim. "It will be three to four small shots within the space of two pages where the two of you are looking Saturday morning domestic. Perhaps this is your first kitchen together, the first time you've ever shared a kitchen, and you've just made love while cartoons played in the background. Now you're hungry, it's winter. The house is warm. Your loungewear is so cozy; it makes you want each other like crazy. It's the loungewear of your babyhood. Everything you touch should be cozy, fun, taken care of. You can go out for the newspaper in this stuff, parade around in it. Understand?" Wolfgang finished speaking as if he'd just finished breathing. He was so resolute that day. Wolfgang noticed he didn't feel at all threatened by Tim, and figured he was fifteen years Tim's senior, at the very, very least.

Tim was the male model for the loungewear shoot. He was having trouble looking Saturday morning domestic, and started getting an erection standing around in his underwear with Mindy. He was supposed to feel as if this underwear, boxer shorts really, made him feel what Wolfgang said New York called *subtly luxurious*. The pose Tim liked best was the one where Mindy sat on the counter and he embraced her from a standing position directly in front of her. The whole thing turned Wolfgang on because all the while he thought of standing that way with Mindy himself. Still, Wolfgang could not help but think that the way Mindy looked had something to do with Helene. He didn't even notice that Tim was grappling with his masculinity in an embarrassing way. When Wolfgang took a woman, he took her by fate, place and indecision, he didn't care how he looked or who saw.

Mindy thought about her hunger, how, though she was not sure she was attracted to him, she hungered for Tim to be even closer. As Tim moved closer, she put her neck back, struck a different pose, a variation of smiles and non-smiles, smirks and laughing head back shots. Then Tim shifted his weight. He could take her right there. Wolfgang believed this would be an easy session if Tim's penis could leave off the erections. Leaning back toward the wall above the kitchen counter, Mindy wanted waffles with whipped cream and raspberries and freshly squeezed orange juice. Tim's arm moved her this way and that. She yearned for hot Darjeeling tea with lemon and honey. "Marry me," Tim said, trying not to laugh after Wolfgang shouted, "Look as though you are getting everything you want, that this is the weekend that begins your life of comfort in these wonderful pajamas." Mindy thought the *Sunday Times*, English tea biscuits smothered in butter, and a comfortable sofa sounded like a good idea, the kind of thought the picture expected of her. Really, she wanted to be overtaken by this easy cape of a house, to make it her own. Mostly, she wished to push her lips against Tim's. She wanted all these things simultaneously, and then her hunger dared her to want none of them.

Anxious again, Mindy could taste tin in her mouth. Looking off at the appliances, she thought back to when her mother used to put a padlock and chain around the refrigerator between meals. She thought of how she could not reach the red box of macaroons that sat on top of the avocado green refrigerator. It was then she felt the hunger spreading to her feet, making them cold, wanting for wool socks. While Wolfgang put more film into his camera, she licked her lips, and Tim tried fighting yet another erection by thinking about Mindy sitting on the toilet.

Wolfgang accidentally dropped the camera while he put more film in because he momentarily got wrapped up in the fact that he didn't have a window with real snow in it, and he believed snow brought forth answers and definition. In the kitchen, the stylist had put fake snow around the windows inside the panes. Nervously and in a sideways concentration, Wolfgang thought of smoking endless joints while sitting on a carpet in a cabin with Mindy. He thought the snow would ritually cleanse him. He liked the dream quality of snow because it made everything appear to be the same, even and white, without any dark shades of gray, except in springtime, which he considered an aggravation of the human spirit, a greening cruelty. No, he liked the certainty and comfort that snow brought, and he wasn't sure fake snow in the windows would bring that same comfort to the shoot.

"Damn it," Wolfgang yelled. "The film's jammed."

Wolfgang sent his Niagara Spray and Starch assistant in blue jeans to go get the other camera, even though the one Wolfgang held in his hands was his favorite.

"Go get some doughnuts, for Christ's sake," Wolfgang told Mindy and Tim, as he shoved the keys to his BMW into Mindy's hands. Even though Wolfgang said he was allergic, Tim and Mindy smoked in his car the whole way to the store.

Back at the copywriter's desk, two hundred miles away in New York, the white-haired copywriter remembered the intrigue of his first house, the freedom and the enclosure of it. How he could watch the whole world from his living room window, and how he could smell the musty familiar scent of it still. He could even remember the way his wife would sit and brush her long hair as she watched television from the sofa by the big picture window that looked out toward the streetlights and the headlights of cars passing by. He could not remember what she was wearing the day they first walked into the house, and somehow this seemed fitting to him as he wrote the line: *What Was She Wearing When?* Because, although the words were supposed to evoke memory, all he could do was think toward the future and how he would master the beautiful Helene and bring her with him into the heart of himself, deep through the staircase of his desire and boredom.

At night, the copywriter dreamt only of Helene, how he would see her in the next catalogue. She would appear to him in his sleep like an angel in a diaphanous white shirt that came down to her knees. How she stood in each different naked pine and white hallway and entranceway with her elbows bent, her hair in flight, everything suspended in a white gauze of light. In his vision, he delighted in how she walked through the thresholds of these intimate spaces in an almost whimsical fashion; he imagined Wolfgang following her with his longing lens, putting whatever he could to testimony. In his dreams, the copywriter felt the presence of her image from this picture not yet taken, and felt every crevasse of Helene's presence as it related to who he knew himself to be during the pure, guarded moments of his escapeful and watched sleep.

Far from New York, over at the supermarket with Tim, Mindy felt she was at a carnival, that survival had come down to this strange, easy living. Usually, she grocery shopped as if it were a hobby, to soothe her boredom and anxieties. As soon as she entered a supermarket she went into a trance, lit up by the aisles of food and the fluorescent lights. Tim walked slightly behind, pretending to be aloof. He looked at whatever she lifted off the shelf as if she were telling him a secret, speaking a language of sustenance to him. The two of them did the same dance every male-female couple in the supermarket seemed to do, the women drawing the men intimately in toward what they had in their hands, toward what would nourish them if they desired to eat it, partake of it.

Dreamy, tired, hungry, she and Tim loaded their cart up with soft cheeses and pumpernickel squares of bread and green apples, ripe mangoes, a pecan coffee cake, sweet cream, and a bright pink package of sugarless chewing gum. At the checkout line, paying the bill, Tim and Mindy looked at each other with the recognition of what it would be like if they were married, sharing in the sacramental decisions of domesticity. Thus, they tried to avoid looking at one another, and instead stared at the cashier's purple-veined left hand as she touched what they had chosen.

Back at the easy white cape, where the sound of the nearby ocean was ripping stones into sand, Helene felt aggravated with Wolfgang's piercing glances. She sat at the dining room table and worked a crossword puzzle. Whenever Wolfgang looked at her, he saw only his mother's female lover in the dark of her lavender-smelling bedroom. She intimidated him. To Wolfgang,

Helene was like the crack of light he let in when he opened his mother's bedroom door after he had wet his bed and needed her help.

"What's the matter? You seem kind of strange lately," Wolfgang said to Helene.

Helene put her pencil down on the table next to the crossword.

"Someone's been dreaming of me. I can feel it," she told Wolfgang.

She stood up, and moved toward Wolfgang, who in turn stood up, and followed Helene, who waved him in her direction.

"Come here. I want to show you something," Helene told Wolfgang, and he followed her up the slippery stairs.

Wolfgang followed Helene as if she were a vision, a camera held tightly in his hand. Helene stopped and then stood in the doorway to the master bedroom, the Dutch lace curtains accented the artificial snow in the window panes behind her. With his camera, Wolfgang focused tightly on her face, and he no longer saw his mother or her lover in Helene, but a woman on the verge of tenderness. He saw that the outline of her face had become softer somehow. Her brown hair a striking contrast to the white creaminess of the entranceway. And Wolfgang began to feel a lust that had the weight of his fifty-four years as he watched Helene bend over to touch her ankle in the light of the easy cape where the sound of the ocean lured him into the house of female desire, and made him a captive in the copywriter's dream of Helene.

Intermezzo

The Holy Ghost
In Flight Over the coastline
of Connecticut

I am the mystery of time producing nostalgia. I am the way dreams inform history. I am the means through which all communication flows, the conduit. I am the moment that builds upon itself until all scripture is fulfilled. I am the moment full as a peony as it breaks out of bud into a fragrant bloom of color.

I am the look of time past and the look of time future. I am the detail in all seen things: the button, the wave, the collar, the cuff, the sky, the man. I am all ages, and the way one age turns into another.

IV

Back to School Issue, Autumn
1999

The bang and clamor of the copper kettle sun, as if hanging off the wall of pure sky—reflected itself against the green, green leaves. Producing red, rust, vermilion-orange, bronze-brown, mango, and banana colored leaves; the sun was asserting itself in days. Leaves and assorted sweaters. Time collapsing into the into. That light on the white houses in the distance, the ivy on the stone of the old school building, and Mindy posed on the swings. All under the sheen and gloss and desire of Wolfgang's lens that made time congeal. Wolgang's lens. A certain heat. A certain light. Wolfgang's third eye. Mindy on the swings with little Caroline, Wolfgang's small niece, on her lap holding on for dear life, laughing.

"Higher! Higher!" screamed the child with wild joy.

"No, no! Not too high!" Wolfgang commanded.

Releasing her bent knees, Mindy reached her toes outward and up. Then backward with the shins (so hard to get the idea at first when one was a child, then becoming second nature), then—Again!—outward and up toward the great divide—heaven from earth. Above, Mindy knew, dwelt the great movement moving her (beyond all the pointing and flexing of her toes, the lengthening and release of her legs). On her cheekbone a small freckle grew, but no one noticed. Her make-up felt heavy upon her small, delicate, pixie's face. Like a layer of sadness, it felt like. But it wasn't sadness exactly, though mostly like it. The sadness on her face was a veil. The sadness she felt had a sweetness to it that was as wide as the motion of the swing itself, the arc of that motion. But it wasn't melancholy, exactly. And it wasn't self-pity. It was just a pure and weighty sadness as beige as face paint in autumn sun, but you couldn't see it through Wolfgang's lens. In his lens the weighty sadness was captured, collected, filtered, and purified like water, made crystalline pure. Made essence. Made memory. The child on her lap was the juxtaposition in the photograph, the elation that exists outside the sadness. The child was sheer simplicity, innocence. For Wolfgang, the child was the relic of the past, the hope for everything good.

"Weeeeee," the child screamed, her hair flying backwards, her small fingers gripping the metal chains of the swings, just above Mindy's hands.

"Terrific! Terrific!" Wolfgang called out, bending his knees deeper.

"We're headed in the right direction!" he said, as he moved quickly around them. Helene swang softly on the swing next to them.

The direction Wolfgang was headed was the late fifties. On this day Wolfgang was looking for 1957, he asked the light to come join him, to marry all memory and expose what was then into the now. Wolfgang, the great director of time's secrets, though he knew not what the secrets themselves were. He was the traffic director of nostalgia, telling the past when to come upon the present in the intersection of time. A choreographer of moments, that was how Wolfgang saw himself. Wolfgang the big-boned photographer. Wolfgang the guy with the entire lady trouble.

But this day was all pearls and sweater sets and cashmere and pleated short wool skirts. Satchels and thick heeled shoes. Ivory buttons and red lined lips. This day was supposed to look like 1957 through the blue tinted lens of time possessed of foreknowledge, of time possessed of itself and made new. Here the small details in zippers and buttons and understated things about the cut and style gave the illusion of now, so that forty years hence what was worn remained a record of how design explained ourselves to ourselves. Cars, Wolfgang always thought of the cars he had seen on display at the Beaux-Arts Musee in Montreal—a history of the automobile. How each era's design spoke to the soul, silently and in private about the meaning of each automobile's time. So much to be said in the smallest curve, color, flourish, sleekness. The history of the world, Wolgang believed, was all right there in such nuances! And now all this silent hysteria for the past, for nostalgia, but always the belief that something way back when was simpler.

"Okay, now let's have Mindy and Helene on the swings. Caroline you go and take a break with Nanny," Wolfgang said.

"Ohhhh, Uncle Wolfy!" the child said, stomping her feet onto the dirt below the swing.

Her Nanny ran right up to her and picked her up.

"Remember what we talked about Caroline," the Nanny said to the child as the two walked away from the set.

Mindy and Helene began to swing again.

"Not in tandem!" Wolfgang shouted. "Slower!"

"No the world is not more complicated now, as nostalgia would have us believe," Wolfgang said to his assistant, as he furiously clicked away at the scene. Not simpler, just different, Wolgang thought as he caught Mindy and Helene on film looking at each other and laughing a laugh both innocent and dark, a laugh full of white picket fences and Vodka martinis. He clicked away. A delivery truck drove loudly by at the moment he clicked this picture of Mindy and Helene as they looked at each other and laughed on the swings, and it startled him and he breathed through his nose. He began to smell something there at the edge of the old college campus by the swings and tennis court and large white tent they'd set up. The oak trees loomed over it all like premonitions, and the light that was let through narrated it's own memory. He was beginning to smell the separation of time into quadrants of before, after, now, and eternity.

Like a tree leaf, like a tree leaf, Mindy thought the sound of her heart was saying as it pumped blood loudly through her chest—like a tree leaf. That's how her heart felt as she swang: like a tree leaf falling into the bronzing cast of sunlight and down into the green of grass. She wasn't entirely sure she wanted to sleep with Wolfgang anymore. No, not sure at all. The way his large body shadowed over her small bones. And his nightmares and cold sweats and fevers. His smells! "What was that smell?" he'd say, deep into the night, as if always chasing after something, hunting down that which he could not see. She couldn't stand it sometimes. Still, he was sweet, the way he was with women, could talk to them and love them so easily, make them feel as if he understood. He seemed so big boned and vulnerable and polite, yet driven, softly angry, full of intense light, the light of a pointillist painting.

Not like the light that shines here, Mindy thought. Not the light on the white house over the bank of the hill beyond the college, Mindy thinking to herself, releasing her bent knees and twisting her swing.

"Around and around!" Wolfgang shouted.

"Lean back more!"

"More!"

And she did, devotedly. More. She let the light and moment move her. Westchester, she was in Westchester again. Westchester! She thought of Katherine Hepburn, in that movie, (which one was it, she couldn't remember) yelling: Westchester, Westchester, we're going to Westchester in that old-fashioned (was it high Boston?) English that no one spoke anymore, except a few white-haired grandmothers. And the lightness Hepburn conveyed of it, the very word. That light. The light and the oak trees moving all time to the beat of bulldozers ruining the landscape. Her heart grew toward the light and the oak leaves as they drifted through the Hudson River air.

Light and time moved differently here, she believed, having grown up in this self-same town. She had swung here as a child. Yes, time lived here in the light silting through the changing oak and maple trees. A past time was kept in the old stately rooms of Sleepy Hollow, in houses that looked over the river, in the parks that held stone walls and views of the bridge at Tappan Zee. She had seen the way the light was kept, preserved not only in memory, but in museums, the Hudson River School Painters—her grandfather had shown them to her—devoted, bald grandfather waiting for her in front of the school once a month on Fridays, leaning gently on the side of his old Mercedes with his cap on, waiting to take her to art museums. That was what the blueprint of Northern Westchester's soul was—she thought—those huge oaks by the Hudson, under which lovers huddle and kiss, as if in paint against the canvas, the blue of sky, the cliffs of the palisades on the other side. Everything painted and real at once—the blanket on the grass, the boats on the water, the river, the stones of Rockwood Park, the grass, that still and quiet love she once felt, all seemed painted (yet real!) was it a Thomas Cole or Francis Silva? Now so many condominiums everywhere, it wasn't the same really, that's why she felt extra excited about the light, which remained, and of course, the oak trees. Now there were so many condos where the woods once were, the woods where she had kissed a boyfriend she loved for the first time, he was married now. That's what this light is, Mindy thought, as she sat on the red strap of the old swing, the softness of the cashmere sweater set against her back was softer than she could bear, the light was as revealing as her loves had been. And always, she thought, the huge great Hudson River sky painted over them, and the trees making the light so much more grand, especially with the smell of autumn in the air.

Wolfgang could smell it from where he was standing, the smell circled him, it was crisp and thick. Autumnally, he felt the weight and heft of it upon Mindy. The weight that wasn't melancholy or self-pity, just a sadness that had to do with the light. At first he thought it came from the direction of Helene. Helene swang beside Mindy. Helene twisted herself around and around and leaned back and laughed. Helene. Helene. She still found the swings liberating, especially late at night, after the bar, she relished sitting on them, watching the night sky open itself from beneath the tender shield and umbrage of leaves. She sometimes brought her dates to the swings across the street from the bar—Murphy's. It was fun to kiss these grown men as they sat beside her, feet dragging on the sandy ground, going back and forth. How she loved waiting for the kiss that might finally send her into the sensual crevasses of a summer evening. But those evenings were fading into the worn corduroy of autumn. She began to wonder what the guys on page forty-two were doing in their oxfords and cable knit sweaters, the guys who usually did handstands on the beach by sand jeeps for the summer catalogue. Gustav, the one with blonde hair. And Paul the one with nice pecs. She'd ask them out for beers later. How nice it would be to always have those two handy, she thought. She hoped sex would build a protective barrier around her, soothe away the past or future that wasn't hers, that was trying to infiltrate her life. That dream, she could feel it!

"Stop, stop, stop it!" Wolfgang yelled.

His face was beginning to turn rosacea red.

"You're giving me a panic attack!" he said to Helene, who suddenly had stopped moving and was staring awkwardly out into space, no longer posing proficiently. Helene had been too deeply in her thoughts. Merely posing as a woman staring into space and out of the dream that Wolfgang tried to capture with his lens. A hinge was coming off the door of Wolfgang's entrance into the world he was trying to make. The swing set. The cashmere and pearls, Mindy's Westchester light, but filtered blue, awash in 1957.

Awash in someone's dream again, Helene felt herself to be just a shadow, a form illuminating the night as if she were a sun that shone only in the dark of night. This very sun, she thought, hot and melding everything into the golden soul of a collective unconscious. And she all pearls and cashmere and pleated wool skirt, all satchel and French twist, a helix of primary blue and white, a schoolgirl lost in the schoolgirl's dream of finally becoming a woman, lipsticked and powerful. The schoolgirl's dream became Helene as it had grown in Helene's very own heart. The smallest detail of Helene's attire provided for the image of the dream realized. The smallest detail.

Like the freckle that appeared on Mindy's nose. Mindy was thinking about Tim. She thought about how when Wolfgang was out of town on a photo shoot in Bermuda with the bikini models and the boys doing handstands in the sand on page forty-two, she had let Tim come and sit beside her on a garden bench at Helene's house. He had come to sit beside her and kiss her on the neck, just below her left ear, and then he walked away. He said nothing to her! And somehow it had seemed more than saying something. She liked simplicity, how it was so accessible and yet inaccessible as well. Oh, the puzzle of it. Oh, the wet kiss of it. She tried not to think too much about it, for when she did it would sprout new full blooms of questions, new beauties and horrors. She didn't have the stomach to get into too much thought about it all. But, oh, she thought anyway! That will-o-the-wisp self. How wonderful he had looked in those snug blue jeans coming through the garden deliberately toward her, ducking under the trellis filled with white clematis, and over the path of stone sewn up with a driven, flowering thyme. He was at once positive and negative space. The icon and the idea behind it. He was of time itself, light's best son. His height and angular face, his sweetness and his two long legs. His manner was all business, but the business had indeed been sweet, unexpected. Not at all like Wolfgang, padding over like a sweet, large bear, always in trouble with the ladies for something or other, making it all worse with his strange and awkwardly timed comments about smells. How did this all happen, anyway? Mindy wondered, as Wolfgang implored her to come back to "Earth! Earth!" The shoot was nearing a big lull.

"Let's try some new moves," Wolfgang said.

"Nanny!" he screamed.

The child's Nanny ran over, slightly out of breath.

"Yes, Mr. Ackerbloom," the Nanny said, slightly nervous

"Wolfgang, call me Wolfgang. No one calls me Mr. Ackerbloom. That would be my father," Wolfgang said.

"Of course," said the Nanny. "What can I do for you?"

"Bring the child back on set," Wolfgang instructed.

In a few minutes the child came running back onto the set with the Nanny and a make-up stylist trailing behind her.

"Helene, you stand up, push Caroline in the swing. Tim, you take Mindy's place on the other swing, and Mindy you stand off in the background, push your hair in front of your face a bit," Wolfgang said.

Everyone moved to their new positions and did as instructed.

"Good, good, keep moving, pushing. There, now," Wolfgang said, as he fired away with his camera.

He wanted to isolate Mindy's distance, and use it as a backdrop.

"Look off into the distance behind you," Wolfgang said to Mindy.

He wanted to make it look as if Mindy were some sort of child of time bringing in new moments, making sure the past receded into it's proper place, back into the shelter of the stand of old pine trees. Pine trees, Wolfgang thought, were the woods that held the haunted past. That's why they were in so many children's stories. He did not want Mindy to look as if she stood watch like a guardian angel. No, she must look like time's child ushering in new moments, passing on the old moments to the wise thickness of the pine trees.

Young Caroline giggled on the swing.

"Underdog! Underdog!" The child yelled, laughing the whole time, showing his perfect, American teeth.

"Great! Excellent!" Wolfgang said, moving from left to right and right to left. He was getting the swift current of time washing over his subjects. The design of the clothing did its part to connect the present to 1957.

This is a great, great job, Wolfgang thought, glad he had dropped out of graduate school to go to briefly cover Nam once he realized he could not be drafted due to a fluttering of the heart. Even if he never did take pictures for AP again, he didn't care. Even if he had hated Nam, had been spooked by the image in his head that would eternally haunt him, he was glad to have had the experience so he could fully appreciate what it was he had with his fashion photography. Still, the image of a young girl chasing the helicopter full of dead GIs that Wolfgang had grabbed a ride out of combat from still haunted him. He had tried to catch a story, and barely left with his life. The picture of that girl still in his heart, the smell of the bodies in the chopper still in his nose. He hadn't been well suited to covering wars, he thought it would make him a man. Riding in helicopters, marching alongside soldiers completely jarred him out of the dream he thought photography was, or should be. He didn't have an instinct for an actual story, he continually found himself in the worse places. He was in love with metaphor, and metaphor walked the runway of fashion, smelling distinctly of lavender and hot lights. The metaphor in Nam was not the metaphor Wolfgang wanted to photograph. What had been in

Nam was beyond metaphor, beyond Mr. Kurtz, it had been quite frankly, beyond Wolfgang, and it had stunk of death.

There was something about working for the fashion industry that made him feel close to something diaphanous, angelic, something that was weighty, winged, and securely in time in a way that recording actual history didn't do for him. With fashion and advertising shoots, he was the one implementing the image that would mark time and say what was stylish. Fashion photography was the documentation of the way human beings thought things should look. As some strange muse told them it should be. That was the beauty of this industry versus the photojournalism and news industry. Plus, the thrill of almost losing your life in the jungle had seemed less romantic once he had actually landed in Saigon in 1969. He was successful with the women there, but that was it. He took portraits of them that had appeared in an anthology of Vietnam era photographs.

Always, women for Wolfgang. In the seventies, when he lived in Greenwich Village, he liked to recite Shakespeare's sonnets to them. It still worked, even with the alcoholic anorexic that he had to photograph in her skimpy underwear last month for a cosmetics billboard. Like a lullaby, he found the sonnets to be, even to the cagiest hearted women of them all. Either it lulled them into his little history-re-writing world, or it cast them out so blindly into the realm of the heat of the sun that the starkness it produced appealed to those who had hired him. A win–win situation lately, or so he had felt. Lately, it seemed as if everything was for sale or owned by a big corporation, and they all wanted their own versions of the world. Wolfgang, the historian! Wolfgang the great! He had never been able to attain this stature, even during his months in Vietnam, finding choppers to ride with for a story. There had been no glory in it for him, only a hallucination that no morning coffee could cure. The perpetual image and stench of running to hop on a chopper loaded with corpses to get the hell out, a small Vietnamese girl chasing him, trying to get on the chopper. Wolfgang would always try to lose this image in the thick silt of the fashion dream, it's heavy boa tickling him back into this life, where he was Wolfgang the Great!

Wolfgang the Historian! He thought to himself again, embarrassed over the egoism he felt upon seeing his finished work. Yes, when all was said and done Wolfgang felt himself to be an explorer, finding, mapping, and settling new worlds for corporations to sell. And money! He had to admit he loved the money, and the stock market that made him more money. And he loved it or didn't care (depending on his mood) that the President fucked lots of blondes with haircuts like Princess Diana, and that no one seemed to give a hoot about stuff like that anymore. It was a New World a coming, and Wolfgang could smell it. He was a long way from that chopper, and the girl chasing him, and his strange desire to set fire to his camera.

One thing he really didn't understand was why all of a sudden children were used like props for photo shoots. He suspected that it had something to do with selling a new kind of family, a new version, updated 1950s family. One of his sisters, Marianne, had begged him to get her child into modeling, and so the child was on the set, usually well behaved, but sometimes a little bossy (like his sister, he always thought).

"Let's get a few shots of the three of you on the swings all close together with Mindy sitting off in the distance behind you drinking a glass of water," Wolfgang said, reloading his camera.

He thought the water had something to do with purity. Only part of Mindy, her hands lifting the cup to her mouth, her long legs, her hair, would be in the photo. It would be cropped.

Mindy sat in the director's chair sipping the water, feeling relieved.

"Talk about something funny to someone off in the distance who the viewer can't see," Wolfgang said.

He thought that left room open for possibility, humor, and imagination. He wanted her to be slightly out of focus, because that's how time comes and goes, sometimes out of focus.

Mindy was glad, because she disliked ice and there was no ice in the water. She loved Europe because she despised ice in drinks. Searchingly, she looked at Tim while Wolfgang looked at him too, but through the Leica's lens. Golden, the world seemed so. The starched white and blue of the clothes against that certain slant of light that was traveling religiously over them and toward and into the winter that the autumn thickness was bracing for. The will of the world's moments were what Wolfgang wanted to saturate the plain of photographic paper with. And love, Mindy, thought, as she looked at him. She did not feel love. Just the sheer weight and tonnage of it could be so awful. A feeling? Yes, love brought a feeling; it was just one she could never name, like that slant of light she loved, so full, so stark, both oppressive and rich. It was the scent of sun against wool.

The light was as full as a mock orange in early summer, that full blossoming and white. *O light, tell me what I want.* That's what she thought. She couldn't tell herself because she was just beginning to know. Pinnionnated, not yet. She was not yet the winged soul that came from living days rightly. No, not yet. But Helene was close to this transcendence. Jealousy! Mindy was looking on, and was having trouble distinguishing posing from life. She wanted Tim. She did not want Helene to have Tim. Bigger and bigger Wolfgang's bottom seemed to her, as she looked on at Tim. Suddenly she could feel Tim's body against hers as she sat in her chair drinking Pellegrino water with no ice. Everything was dragging itself into her. *It's Westchester,* she thought.

Westchester does this to me. The past skimming the surface like schooners navigating the Hudson in Francis Silva's " The Hudson at Tappan Zee." The quietude and spaciousness of the water there, her whole soul felt that long, that fluid. The days felt that way, too, where the past was welded on so firmly to the present, and the present seeming so like the view of the Hudson at Tappan Zee—a beautiful, pure thing made purely out of elements meeting the moment, a merging full of a strange pigmented paint made equally of vision and light and being. There was a bridge now at the spot Silva painted, and Mindy had watched the lights there at night from a hill by the bank. She liked to stay there all night watching the tugboats pull in day. She could feel the lips of her first boyfriend still in the Hudson light that reached her face. It was the light from the Hudson that originated here in this part of New York where even the oaks seemed inoculated with a primary life, and the river still and busy bringing the past along wherever it went—an eggshell blue past, thick with the attention of the Hudson School Painters. It was a blue hue that found itself even on walls in drawing rooms all up and down Scarborough and Sleepy Hollow.

And always dear old, bald Grandfather, Mindy thought, and his sweet museums. How she had loved his pipe tobacco, that scent in the leather seats of his car and in the weave of his Harris Tweed. Dear Grandfather waiting for her when the bell of school would ring out—Done! In this light there would always be school, and still that rancid smell of wool sweaters in sun. She gave way to it, as her body gave way to the very chair she sat in. But she did not know if she could give way to Tim, though she realized she wanted him. In this light she felt herself to be a bibliography of the past, a list of sources, a book to be fingered through. She was compiled, but not complete.

Not complete. Different from the surface completeness Wolfgang was composing for the photo shoot. A surface completeness that could convince one it ran deep, that it had a well and a source that ran from the water of Narcissus reflecting right into Wolfgang's third eye. Mindy could hear him humming, softly singing, *your daddy's rich and your Ma's good looking*. Splendid in her theme cashmere and pearls, Helene looked full of Tim. Tim in his powerful stance. Tim in his close up. Tim in his broadcloth shirt. Mindy's jealousy grew.

And sweet little Caroline who should have been in school, instead was a small girl wishing to be Helene, her small nose rubbing against Helene's nose. A family? This was what Wolfgang wanted, the idea of the hip, smart, beautiful family—life made perfect through the lens of his Leica. The shoot kept making everyone think of whatever it was they thought. Mindy's jealousy began to have stamina. And Wolfgang was not thinking of Mindy.

Snow. Wolfgang was wishing for snow again. He didn't understand it, but this light made him think purely of snow. In favor of it absolutely, snow for him was a purity that numbed him into feeling all right with the world. For him the lens of his camera was a distance to traverse. Something that brought ascension or decimation, something to be monitored, conquered, watched. The slow shutter speed of his heart was directly related to winter. *That certain slant of light* for him held the weightiness of which Emily Dickinson spoke. That mystery. Miss Emily, as Wolfgang called her. When he was younger, back before he went to cover Nam, he'd briefly thought he wanted to be a poet. But day after grueling day he'd written nothing, only leafed through *Life Magazine* photographs, and spent time in the darkroom or looked at photographs by Cartier- Bresson and Irving Penn. Though he loved Miss Emily and all the longhaired, braless girls at the coffee house poetry readings, he loved the idea that cameras were a faster way of seeing, and he was off to Nam to document what he saw, to tell a story with a morbid, death poetry of lens and fearlessness. And when he came back, there were still American women. Women everywhere, in sets of two if he had wanted. Carnivorous, he thought it his undoing.

He eventually moved to New Hampshire with a stripper he met at a poetry reading near NYU. She'd had a job on the county fair circuit back in the early seventies. Wolfgang felt at home at the fair and photographed all the strippers and carnival ladies, compiling them into a book called "At the Fair" for which he became well known in certain avant-garde circles composed partly of trust-fund pot heads and real starving artists.

Wolfgang had four children with the carnival stripper, all out of wedlock. An old thought from the old days, he thought his love needed no legislation, no recognition by any power other than his own libido. Why sew oneself so needlessly to another, he'd thought. But now his old friends had begun marrying in case they died—who would get their social security? Things had become practical after all. He, himself, had come to carrying a picture of his mother in his wallet. A lovely mother dressed in 1940's floral dress, standing in front of Ackerbloom's Meats in Madison, Wisconsin. Oh, mother, when he thought of her his right eye began to twitch.

"Take ten," he called out. His right eye was getting tired, and he was beginning to realize the other side of 1957.

"Uncle Wolfy," Caroline said, coming to stand near her uncle, and then kicking him in the shin.

"I was having fun! You ruined it!" Caroline said, crossing her arms and pouting.

Wolfgang tickled the child under the armpit with his index finger. She stuck her tongue out at him. How like his sister she looked, Wolfgang thought. He was a large man who didn't mind bad behavior from youngsters.

"Honestly Caroline, leave your poor Uncle alone," the Nanny's voice cried out, moving quickly toward the child on the set from the big white tent where she had been sitting.

"Time for a clothing change," Wolfgang said.

"I think this set's a wrap."

"Cookie first!" Caroline called out from the arms of her Nanny, who had picked her up and was whisking her off to costume change.

"The nice assistant has some lemonade for you, Caroline," the Nanny said.

"But I don't like lemonade!" Caroline wailed from the Nanny's arms.

The Nanny put the child down and grabbed her hand and started walking her toward Neil to get the glass of lemonade.

"Come, come, Caroline, you don't want to get dehydrated and you know perfectly well you like lemonade. Why just yesterday you spoke only of lemonade for a full half hour on the car ride home."

Neil hoped he wouldn't drop anything. The Nanny was coming his way. He thought Caroline's Nanny had a particularly nice ass, and wanted to be as accommodating as possible to get in her good graces. His line of attack was to keep the child well behaved and not a bother, so that the Nanny would think him helpful. He had overheard the Nanny talking earlier about how Caroline loved lemonade, and he quickly decided to supply some for the child. He had also stocked up on gummy bears and caramels.

"Well aren't you thoughtful!" the Nanny told Neil, thinking Neil was way too skinny for his height and could use some lemonade and gummy bears himself. Although she herself was ten pounds overweight with a hooknose and short dyed blonde hair, she secretly hoped to be "discovered" on the set and catapulted into mail order fame. By whom she might be discovered, she did not know. Like Veronica Lake, that's who she thought she looked like in her best moments, but anyone honest and heartless enough could surely tell her otherwise. She looked nothing like Veronica Lake, not even in her fantasies about herself.

Helene could tell the Nanny was lit with yearning. She could sense it in all of the Nanny's pronouncements and movements. Opportunist, Helene thought the first moment she set her eyes on the Nanny, but kind and dumbly sweet and good enough to be a Nanny. Helene couldn't stand all the shopping bags from the Gap that the Nanny always had. Helene believed the Nanny tried too hard to be beautiful, and that all that trying made her look plastic. She believed the Nanny smelled too much of the mall, of hot pretzels, and Calvin Klein's Obsession.

Everyone wanted to be beautiful, Helene thought from her green director's chair looking at the Nanny out of the corner of her eye. Why some were deemed beautiful and others so-so or completely ugly, Helene did not know. Weren't there two types of angels that had roamed the earth, she thought, the earth way back when, when horrible angels who had loved earth's women begot them troubled and troubling children? Those children brought trouble, but they also brought a certain beauty, Helene thought.

"Steel Belly! Oh, Mr. Steel Belly!" The child began to call out loudly from her chair with lemonade in one hand and gummy bears in the other.

"Oh, Uncle Steel Belly! Where are you!" the child called out to Wolfgang, that was her pet name for him. He let her punch him in the stomach, which she said was made of steel.

She called out for him again. But she could not find her uncle.

Wolfgang was off, sitting in his BMW with the air-conditioning on (he still yearned for winter, it's calming snow)

69

eating a Whitman's Sampler and listening to Louis Prima, having a private moment. His right eye was still twitching slightly from thinking of his Mother, though he didn't realize his eye twitched every time he thought of his mother. Mother standing in front of Ackerbloom meats circa 1952. Beautiful Mother saved from the war. The love of Madison, Wisconsin's East Side. The beauty of his Mother attacked his soul as if his soul was nothing more than a bialy crumb on the sidewalk in the sun surrounded by ants. Yes, ants on all sides of life's poor beauty!

And the beauty of Mindy, Wolfgang thought, as he ate one chocolate after another. The chocolates were beautiful, too. He was beginning to feel better and the music saying "zooma-zooma" each time he put a candy in his mouth. Bite and see was not Wolfgang Ackerbloom's eating style when dealing with a Whitman's Sampler. He did not peck at his food. Especially candy. Especially not women. He believed a healthy appetite was a good sign, a sign that all was right with the world. He believed moderation was a product of puritanical thinking. The body knows when it's finished, was Wolfgang's creed. He thought of Mother watching him almost throw up from four helpings of noodle kugel. "Enough already!" his mother would say, "no one eats four helpings of Kugel, you'll get gas!" Still when he'd introduce a girlfriend to his mother for the first time, Mother would inevitably recount the time when Wolfgang was ten and ate a whole chocolate cake in one sitting and she didn't stop him. Then she'd say, "don't forget, he's a night eater, he sneaks into the kitchen at three a.m. and eats whatever you were planning to serve for dinner the next day! Be careful to hide food for guests."

Food and women and the wide aperture of his lens—that was Wolfgang's beauty, his scope. And always within him the image of his Mother at Ackerbloom's weighing steaks and salamis. And his first photograph of her, the one he carried in his wallet, dog-eared, circa 1952. He had been six years old when he took the photograph when his father, on a whim, allowed him to take the picture with his Uncle Lenny's new camera. Uncle Lenny the newspaperman from Chicago, smoking cigars and drinking Gibson martinis. Uncle Lenny who taught Wolfgang all his best moves, with women and with life. Uncle Lenny telling racetrack stories and bringing comic books. Uncle Lenny who gave Wolfgang his start taking pictures for the *Chicago Tribune*. Beautiful Uncle Lenny who had told him not to try and be a hero by taking an assignment in Nam, and then later helped get him back on track with a fashion industry connection in New York.

Beauty, Helene thought as she tapped on Wolfgang's window, was a measure of some sort of purpose. But what about deformities, she always wondered; especially now seeing Wolfgang with the chocolates, she thought the chocolates a deformity, something that should be resisted. She tried to be pure, pure of sugar, pure of dairy foods, pure of shopping malls. Those people who might have been beautiful, but ruined by mercury poisoning, what about them, she wondered? The Nanny always made her think about deformity, oddly enough. She imagined a heartbreaking catalogue shoot where survivors of mercury poisoning modeled all these nice clothes. What would that be like she wondered? She knew not what it meant, the differences between beauty and ugliness. It was a code for something, she suspected. But still she felt the swirling and settling of a dream around her. She was getting a migraine from it, the careening white moths of another ocular disturbance. She knocked on Wolfgang's window again.

"Wolfy, got a Percocet?" she asked.

"I've got a migraine to die for."

Wolfgang let open the electric window and held the box of chocolates up.

"Sorry babycakes, only these suckers," he said.

"No thanks, I don't do chocolate," Helene said.

She couldn't see his eyes. He was wearing his Ray-Ban aviator sunglasses from twenty-five years ago. She didn't like when people spoke to her with their sunglasses on. She trusted only the eyes. A pressure was landing on her, and the day wasn't over yet. Earlier, leafing through her British *Vogue* an advertisement had challenged her to BLOOM! There were flowered hats and dresses blooming all over the page. A beauty made and a beauty sold. That was what she'd been quietly becoming for some time now. Her mother, years ago when they had been living on the commune, said her beauty would be distorted if she took up this modeling business. Even her sister, now a well-known spiritual advisor to the rich and famous warned her that hers was a gossamer winged beauty, one that dreams could slowly fray. Still she thought about that ad to Bloom! But she needed codeine for the migraine that the dream she felt around her was bringing on. She'd have to settle for an aspirin.

"Let me walk you back to the set," Wolfgang told her handing her a bottle of aspirin from his glove box. He put the bottle in her hands, something else also passed between them, but neither was sure exactly what it was. No gossamer winged thing was he—Wolfgang Ackerbloom getting out of his car, yanking up his chinos as he walked with Helene, back toward the tent under which Mindy was sitting, getting her make-up retouched.

Wolfgang walked up to Mindy, touched her wrist with the tips of his fingers, but began to think of Helene. It was a softness Mindy did not know he was capable of. She'd been thinking of Tim, though she knew if she was on a Tim-free diet, she should not shop at the Tim-Mart. No, she should not. But to change the track of thought her mind ran on sometimes proved to be too damned difficult. She hadn't discovered yet that it was as simple a matter as making a decision to stop thinking about something when it showed up wanting to be thought about. Being happy, she hadn't yet realized, was basically a choice. She believed in non-choice. Wolfgang wanted his life to converge with hers the way his lens did with light and subject. He wanted always to make a kind of truth with his camera. He was always diving for the great ball that life threw, and off in the distance Wolfgang could see a gaggle of men and women playing volleyball. The guttural laughs of the men carried on the wind. So much effort, Wolfgang thought, to put into something, just to hit a ball over the lousy net. Poor drudges, Wolfgang thought, their middle aged bravado reduced to this—alumni volleyball.

All of them so sheep-like, routinely pummeling an innocent ball over a tall net. People must constantly need entertainment for a game like volleyball to have been invented, he thought. He remembered shooting pictures of the troops on the beach, and he remembered thinking how stupid it was to be spending what might be one's last moments hitting a ball over an idiotic net. One minute you're mindlessly hitting a ball over a net, the next minute your dead. Unbearable. Why things always had to come down to gamesmanship or a metaphor of gamesmanship completely eluded him. Eluded him in a way his feelings for Mindy eluded him on some days.

But this feeling he had for Mindy, surprisingly, was beyond feeling the need of entertainment. He had hoped it wouldn't come to this with Mindy, him needing her in a way he hadn't expected, beyond gamesmanship. Usually, Wolfgang believed one should not take things too seriously. He stood with his hand still on Mindy's perfectly manicured hand. He could sense her love was as cool as the rush of walking into an air-conditioned theater in July. Good at first, but after awhile it made one too cold. No, passion was not heat exactly, but the constant movement and accumulation of heat in specific places. He moved his hand to her knee where the light lay, and it seemed as if the clothes she was wearing for the next shot were flimsy. The color of her chemise was the color of pale orchises, a matronly color, the favorite color of Wolfgang's Mother, Hannah Ackerbloom. The flounce of the shirt above Mindy's bronzed breast made Wolfgang think of how unearthly women are, how other.

Nothing was ever as it seemed to be, or so Hannah Ackerbloom used to tell Wolfgang. And that's why he loved Mindy. That's what he found interesting about life lived behind the camera. Everything was really just a paradox-headache.

He leaned over and kissed Mindy squarely on the lips.

"Why so sulky?" he said to her.

"I'm not!" she protested. She wanted to say she was merely thinking about Tim, but couldn't. She felt slightly mortified, and wasn't sure what to do about anything anymore.

"Only one more session over by the old administration building and then we'll call it quits for the day," Wolfgang said.

"I need a bath," Mindy said.

"I'll give you a lift back to the city," Wolfgang said. "But I have to drop Caroline and the Nanny off in Scarsdale first."

Scarsdale, Mindy thought. She was in no mood for Scarsdale, or for being asphyxiated by the Nanny's Calvin Klein perfume on the twenty-minute car ride.

"Or you can catch a ride with Helene, and meet me later at my place, I'll cook."

"You know that's my weakness," Mindy said.

Wolfgang could make pancakes so thin, so good, they made Mindy briefly concerned that she might have to join Overeater's Anonymous. There was something holy, communal about them; the way powdered sugar dusted them in the same way the powdered sugar has dusted every pancake since the recipe was created. Wolfgang's pancakes had a long Dutch history. His mother had lived in Laren, outside Amsterdam, and had escaped to America months before the Nazi's came marching in. Her family had run the village pancake house there. Wolfgang had promised to take Mindy there someday.

"It's still there," he told her. "You can sit inside or outside, the place is heated by the cooking irons, and you can still watch the old men perform heavenly alchemy, turning ordinary flour into the food of the gods."

Just as the light itself was an offering to the gods, so were Wolfgang's pancakes. While the pancake house was still there, after the war it was never returned to Hannah Ackerbloom's family. Those who had not escaped to Wisconsin were butchered elsewhere by the Nazis in deathcamps.

And despite that history, Wolfgang saw how at the moment he thought of the pancake house, the light was perfect for the next sequence. He didn't want to miss it, and the light helped 1957 begin to emerge more strongly from his third eye.

"Time's a wasting!" Wolfgang said, and he left Mindy for his camera.

His assistant followed him, all arms and legs, nervous energy, for he had been busy at work readying everything. He wanted to do whatever Wolfgang thought was right.

A hairstylist was chasing young Caroline with a styling brush, but the young child wouldn't stand still, she only wanted to try on a pair of size seven patent leather pumps with lilac satin lining, featured on page thirty-two of the catalogue. Once Caroline had the shoes on she became more tractable, and her hair was perfectly brushed. The other models were ready, although Mindy wondered where Tim was. She didn't see him anywhere, and she was just absolutely praying that he wasn't off with the guys who do handstands on the beach on page forty-two of the summer catalogue. Instead, she felt Wolfgang looking at her. Every time Wolfgang came near her lately she felt either guilty or lustful. The only place she wanted to be was in her mind's eye, thick in the foliage of a fantasy of Tim. She thought back to the garden at Helene's, the thyme sewing the slate path together with it's white flowering, and Tim walking toward her. And then that kiss! Wolfgang couldn't kiss that way if he had taken lessons! But she stayed on with Wolfgang anyway like a faithful memory stays on, continually remaking and distorting itself.

Tim wasn't like Wolfgang at all, yet he did have that same sort of masculine daring and joviality that came in handy at business cocktail parties. He had a personable manner that greeted people with a tender hand on their back and a hundred questions about themselves. His hand on any woman's back in a just so manner that could feel the closure of her bra strap. Wolfgang had learned this technique from his own Mother, by years of watching her as she greeted her female friends at holiday parties back in Madison circa 1957.

Far from the 1957 Wolfgang wanted to evoke here. No he wanted to seal that memory up so tightly and flatly that no part of it would bulge out. He was looking for Beat, though it was not Beat exactly, more of a revisionist, capitalistic conception of Beat. It was the way people not from that era perceived Beat. He wanted to land his vision somewhere in this jungle of stance, but he had to land in it and find where it lived without any technology or night vision. He thought the look he wanted had something to do with the slink and tangle of black and white photos of French lovers by the Seine, but with the light of now. He wanted a startling innocence in a jaded world. He wanted this spread to show the complex and circuitous route of all-will-end-well despite the world, despite the ravishment of time upon soul.

When he sold it to the business dudes, he used slightly different language. He had not wanted to scare them, but he knew the Creative Director understood what he wanted. The head copywriter as well. Mindy and Tim and Helene may or may not have understood, but Wolfgang would mold them into the narrative he wanted. The scene's set was in front of the stone and ivy administration building. Wolfgang needed the models on the granite stairs that lead up to shiny glass doors with gold lettering that was peeling. He believed Tim should be coming out of those doors any minute. He needed the motion of a door closing behind Tim, those beautiful glass doors with the word administration in gold lettering peeling, the admin—on one side of the open door the—istration on the other.

Wolfgang decided the child should lead by standing on one of the stairs below. Mindy should stand on the stairs as if she'd come out the doors a second ahead of Tim. He told them to hold hands, Mindy slightly in front of Tim. Wolfgang had the story written in his head, the Administration meant it was a city hall building not a school building, a place where the two were married. Though they are just married, all time would be with them. The child they'd have in a few years would be represented by Caroline on the steps of the building waiting for them, glancing back, smiling.

So Mindy stood in her first position as if she'd just come out of the door with Tim following closely behind her. But Mindy was not feeling quite herself, and she supposed she was more like a representation of herself. But the light was killing her, not that it was bright, but that it was reaching some part of her sadness that revealed to her that she wished this scene to be the truth, not just the subject for the eye of Wolfgang's camera. She wanted this fantasy to be real. She just wanted to be close enough to Tim, without Wolfgang's light, or time, or penetrating eye. Mostly, she feared Wolfgang would see this desire in her and distort it, have it stand for something other than what it was. She wanted Tim. And Wolfgang captured it. He made it part of his jungle, the one where he must find the truth that appeals to every consumer, world weary and waiting to be drenched in something that is of another world.

Definitively, Wolfgang could feel Mindy's silent narrative coming right down the middle of space and time, making its entrance through his lens and into the belly of his soul. His lens attached itself to some invisible helix that distorted truth in a lovely way. Resolutely, he seduced and undressed time with his Leica. He was some wandering angel's progeny, the great-great-great grandson of one of those horrible earth roaming angels that devoured human women with their light, lust, and earthly lack. He felt that human desire mixed with the heavenly within himself, and for those moments behind the open and release of shutter, Wolfgang believed he had fallen into the great muse's arms and was being held there.

"Mindy, move more toward the right. Good, good!" Wolfgang called out, all the world his to control, at least for this one fraction of a moment.

"Tim. Good, but stay back one more small pace from Mindy. Hold something back from her. Hold back! More! Okay, stop!"

"Now everyone let's take it from the top, everyone in their first positions," Wolfgang said, thinking how perfect the light was, and how the ivy on the building was adding to the interest of the slight shadows. Shadows of a Roman sensibility, he thought. Visions of Roman Holiday with Gregory Peck and Audrey Hepburn haunted Wolfgang with the realization that he would never get exactly what he was after. But he thought, if he was really lucky he might be able to sneak up on a bit of that feeling here at the scene that was the temple shrine to what he was trying to evoke, 1957 crisp and clear and brand new in it's oldness. Wolfgang wanted to give it a bit of the feeling of the old movies he still loved. The granite of the steps seemed Roman in a stately way, full of empire, brimming with

Republic. For him, the way Mindy stepped down the stairs slightly ahead of Tim, but still close, could be an emblem of honesty, of the purity of two people together. The movement he wanted from Mindy was a high-stepped lingering; from Tim he wanted a self-assured waiting. Resolutely, Wolfgang believed the dance should be the regular push and pull of the sexes, yet he wanted the shot to linger in the way nothing cares for us so we must somehow deeply care for one another. Job's story at it's core base. But Job's story Disneyfied and overcome by the salve of a recognizable sexiness that lingers in some early marriage where youth's still natureless dream informs each moment. Wolfgang wanted to capture the distinct angle of love remaining jaunty and alive in the still motion of now, before now turned unrecognizable.

Looking at Tim and Mindy walk down the administration steps with young Caroline walking ahead of them, a blur of jumper and golden hair, high on too much candy and attention, Wolfgang felt certain that it was true, that it took precisely two seconds to fall in love with the world when the light was like this. In silent patriotic prayer above it all the flag jutted out from the side of the Administration building, flapping into the thick air painted of a Hudson River School eggshell blue, a museum quality sky. Wolfgang's third eye clicked away mining the surface, always trying to go one layer deeper into the painting of now as he tried to find the place that would lie and say: It's 1957. He was looking for a spark of that year hiding in the now. His lens scanned for that spark and that lie. What he found was a lie in Mindy's eyes. She didn't love Wolfgang, just as Wolfgang's Mother had not loved his father.

Then, Mindy strode down the stairs, again and again. Like Sisyphus, she dragged her hidden desire for Tim up and down the stairs. She had to click and drag the now back to a specific point in time until she hit the vanishing point at which she disappeared and became everything Wolfgang wanted to capture on film. She twisted her head back slightly to look Tim in the eyes. She let his glance erase her, every text she held tried to delete itself. She had not felt this way with him in the shoot in the kitchen for the winter catalogue. But back then she had been thoroughly dug into Wolfgang as if she were a weed tangled into the thick shrubbery roots of him. She had not noticed then the way Tim's shadow cast not darkness upon her but an oneiric lightness. (And Helene under the tent still and jolted by the dream someone was dreaming of her. That cage! That strange, senseless surge!)

And Tim looked right back at her with an immediacy as thick as time itself. To walk a little behind her made him feel self-conscious, and he couldn't hide it. There was a lot he was having trouble hiding on the set, Wolfgang thought looking at Tim, remembering suddenly the shoot in the kitchen for the winter catalogue. He remembered the *Remember When* headline. Wolfgang thought the tension between Tim and Mindy was good. It was the 1957 desire for moving ahead that was contained in the end part of every decade. It was the desire to stay forever linked, attached to what came before, but also to elapse, turn into the new. And as with all time, Wolfgang had his small niece Caroline lead, lead the older ones down the stairs, as she announced a beginning, a thawing, a change.

He wished he could use black and white film to capture it all. Sometimes he felt black and white was like a microscope. But even with the scene in color, Wolfgang could still capture the elemental honesty that Mindy was in love with Tim. The plain fact stuck in the well of his camera, deep on the film, stored there like an untapped memory. Wolfgang would fully see it later, but for now he was lost in the maze of finding 1957. When he arrived at it, he would know, he would feel it, smell it, the crypt of the past life opening up.

And he was beginning to smell it in the flounce of Mindy's lilac chemise that she wore under the black suit. It was in the pearl bracelet and necklace that she wore against her lightly bronzed skin. It was in the smocked dress redesigned slightly and made in blue velvet that Caroline wore. She strode down the steps in her Mary Janes made new with a slightly stacked heel. Everything was an old style but someone had said: *Make it New!* Wolfgang thought Ezra Pound's dictum had been used on the fashion industry, slightly distorted. Everything seemed new, but it was really old.

"Keep walking Caroline. Smile. High, big steps, that's a girl," Wolfgang called out to his niece, his voice cracking and higher than usual.

Wolfgang was pacing back and forth, jumping. Sideways, his steps were. To any onlooker he might look like he was doing the agility section of the Presidential Physical Fitness test. But he was working, and thinking about Ezra Pound, which was distracting him, that damn fascist! He thought that had Pound not been such a fascist Apple Computer might use him for one of their *Think Different* ads. He could imagine a bedraggled and bearded Pound with the blurb *Think Different* over his shiny, magazine head. Old Pound thinking of metro stops and black boughs. He was sure the industry these days could re-work Pound to make him marketable and sell stuff no one really needed. He thought Pound might be a good way to sell rap music to the so-called gothic youth market. But right now, Pound was definitely not a cultural youth icon.

Wolfgang's other sister Rita had recently been fired from a small, New England liberal arts hippie school for teaching Pound to her students. She had assigned his book *The ABC of Reading* for she had been desperate—they all wrote complete and utter crap about homeless derelicts and heroin addicts, and didn't really give a rat's ass about what anyone before 1967 had to say, except maybe Ginsberg and Keroauc and Burroughs, to the rest they simply cried, *White Males!* Even the white males at the school did not want to be allied with white males. They weren't even interested in Dickinson or Whitman. Somehow it didn't matter that Ginsberg, Kerouac and Burroughs were all white males.

His sister had tried to stay out of the political aspects, but Pound had been one of the masterminds of twentieth century poetry. When she talked about Emily Dickinson her students completely tuned-out, not interested. Her students were the people who would graduate and then quickly come into some money from their parents, move back to New York and wear black garments from this self-same catalogue that Wolfgang shot. The catalogue appealed to the women and it told some story they seemed to be interested in, more than those stories in his sister Rita's Literature course. Though these students could read, image was their true language. His sister, an avid fan of Garrison Keillor, said she liked his description of her kind of students the best, "academically challenged children of financially gifted parents." Yes, Wolfgang thought, his sister was a Midwesterner through and through, and if there were a poster of Garrison Keillor she would have it up in her classroom, just as she used to have a poster of John Lennon in her pink, canopied bedroom back at their parents in Madison. Not only that but she was deeply religious, had become evangelistic. Wolfgang had taken pictures of her and her friends from Jubilee Church doing their prayer walks, which consisted of walking around town in an organized, methodical fashion and praying quietly in front of each house on each block of town until everyone in town had been prayed for. His sister loved Garrison Keillor and Ezra Pound, but hated the devil. Wolfgang was sworn to secrecy to never tell anyone his sister cried every time Garrison sang his introduction song about onions. This particular aspect of his sister nauseated him, but still it was a sweetness that gave him an understanding, it was part of the internal mechanism that made him so sympathetic to women who were not his sister, but equally silly and fragile and smart and full of a humble religious fervor. Even the old ladies loved Wolfgang; he knew how to play old church music on the piano and could play all the hymns. His hands were beautiful piano playing hands, almost like women's hands. His mother had made sure he could play Christian hymns, after arriving from Europe and settling in Wisconsin, she joined the Lutheran church (of which her husband was already a member) in an attempt to lose all her Jewishness, which she feared would one day get her and the surviving family killed. They were the only Lutheran's to eat kugel and gefilte fish, and talk loudly and argue at dinner. Wolfgang was a Jew by birth, but raised in the Lutheran church playing hymns.

His hands firmly on the Leica, all these thoughts and images whirled about him and in him. The shutter let light in again and again. Wolfgang captured Mindy, captured the time that was holding her.

"Shit. Oh, excuse me Caroline," Mindy said, grabbing her ankle. She was holding onto the railing with her other hand. She had twisted her ankle badly. The shoot stopped to let real life in, Mindy with her hurt ankle. Lovely, even with her nose curled up, her mouth drawn in pain. Tim was the first to assist her, and Wolfgang knew this did not bode well for him. He sensed a closeness he was not part of. Tim and Mindy's life was speeding ahead of his. He could smell it! He could smell Tim and Mindy's life together emerging, it had a sweet gardenia like scent, like the perfume Mindy wore. Their desire for each other was producing a floriferous scent, just as his mother's love had produced that lavender scent.

"What's that smell?" Wolfgang asked his assistant.

"What smell?" his nervous assistant answered, hoping Wolfgang wasn't blaming him for passing gas.

"Never mind!" Wolfgang said. He could smell the gardenia scent of Mindy, of love lost, wafting about in the autumn air.

"I'll be all right, Tim. It's fine. Never mind," Mindy was saying still on one foot, as Tim held the other ankle in his hands, bowed down before her.

Little Caroline sat on the stairs with her chin in her hands looking bored.

"I'm hot!" she said.

"Were almost there, sweetie," Wolfgang told the child, as if he were walking the whole bunch of them through a jungle, through their lives converging into a place that housed a divine image, the grail.

Mindy's pain proved valuable to Wolfgang, in it he could find the place he was looking for, and with each shutter release he began to understand the gardenia scent as the essence of a new love slowly coming to the surface of things. The scent began to permeate the scene, and Wolfgang knew he was losing Mindy to Tim. Autumn was closing in on him, and hope balanced itself on the back of reality and slipped off. The oak tree began to shape the sky with its thickness, reconfiguring the love in Wolfgang's heart.

When Mindy's ankle felt better and she came down the steps and turned to look at Tim, she did so with such loveliness, with such a simplicity Wolfgang thought he might choke on his chewing gum. Her look summed up the weight of the poetry that narrated a prayer book. Wolfgang saw his fear tremble into desire. He caught Mindy casting herself onto Tim, onto the world. And the world changed because of this ever so slightly, like a windowpane collecting the fog of breath. And then suddenly it was 1957 and Wolfgang was almost eleven years old, and he felt this feeling back then too, a threshold that said you are forsaken. The world was reintroducing itself to the world because something had changed. The world tinged with change and a small fear that lingered at its core. One thousand story lines converged to make the moment that Wolfgang captured and deposited into his Leica. And all the while Helene under the tent practiced her breathing meditation, breathing through time's rustle. She could feel the change too, something had shifted, and she could feel someone's dream life writing itself more deeply upon her. It made her feel as if someone was looking over her shoulder, but when she turned no one was there, just a few leaves rustling in from another place, another scene.

As she drew the air into her lungs and tried then to empty her thoughts with her breath, she felt like, for the moment at least, a woman solidly inside time. Fully, she could feel the way the day rested upon her. She believed a great and mighty muse constructed the nuances that made us. And Wolfgang felt it too, and knew he must try to capture the image of the dream, the unfillable yearning, the unquenchable lack. Images stalked him just as much as he stalked them before the moment died and was gone, leaving only a tenderness.

And the photo that ended up on page forty-seven of the Back to School Catalogue was filled with the shards of dreams that informed these lives. Just as the trees barely green desired the summer that fell so quickly away, so Wolfgang began to feel a longing for the past. He felt it. The thread of 1957, he thought, was still attached to him with it's sheer, invisible silk. 1957 was the year they spent the summer in the Upper Peninsula of Michigan, he and his sisters, his mother and father, and their friends the Gordons.

Eva Gordon was his mother's best friend, and she was married to Frank Gordon, Professor of Botany at the University of Wisconsin. She had grown up in Bermuda, the daughter of an outcast British Naval Officer and his fun-loving wife. Eva was a third cousin of Frank's, who had married her under arranged terms. Everyone agreed that Frank was basically a sleaze, but no one could ever put their finger exactly on what was amiss. Eva was extravagant and spent a lot of Frank's money, which he had plenty of, having inherited it from his father. Part of his sleaze, according to Wolfgang's sister Rita, was his reputation for sleeping with undergraduates, whom he would invite to cocktail parties at his house.

Frank Gordon had befriended the Ackerbloom's over their delicious sausages, which he bought from Ackerbloom Meats weekly. Frank Gordon believed in fresh meat in an almost religious way, as did Roman Ackerbloom, who had steaks shipped up from the Chicago area yards at least twice a week. Frank Gordon saw some of himself in Roman Ackerbloom, who was an honest wheeler-dealer with a shameless sympathy for the ladies.

Yes, 1957, Wolfgang remembered, was the year the Gordons went on vacation with the Ackerblooms to the Upper Peninsula. It had rained a lot that summer and Frank and Mr. Ackerbloom fished a lot anyway, or when it rained too hard they went to the pub. Sometimes Wolfgang would accompany them fishing, but was not allowed to go with them to the pub. Some days he'd stay inside with the women. The women baking and washing out lingerie and hanging their undergarments out to dry on the screened-in porch on the wooden accordion clothes hanger. Wolfgang would play Chinese checkers out there with his sisters Rita and Marianne. He could still feel those rain-drenched days, even now almost thirty years later. The way every emotion he felt then at the cabin seemed filled with a foreboding musty smell. To this day, whenever Wolfgang felt depressed he swore his skin smelled of must. He could still remember his mother and Eva Gordon in the kitchen smoking cigarettes, drinking black coffee, and playing gin rummy and falling in love. Even then, at almost eleven years old he could see that as plainly as the rain-drenched summer of 1957. He could see it but his sisters couldn't. They thought he was crazy when he said, "Look Mother and Mrs. Gordon are falling in love." Even then he had a certain clarity of vision.

For Wolfgang Ackerbloom the year 1957 was the point at which propriety began to permanently recede. It was the year his vision expanded from the either/or realm of black and white thinking. As he looked at Mindy, Tim and Caroline trying to reproduce this era made new, he couldn't help thinking about that rainy summer in the UP when his vision turned to color. He would always remember his Mother in her terry cloth romper and Mrs. Gordon in her French striped sailor shirt and capri pants, the two of them picking up and discarding their rummy hands with such intensity and vigor, that Wolfgang always understood it as a metaphor for their physical love.

"Uncle Wolfy Belly!" Caroline yelled to him, as he began to put away his camera, and the film, and the memory of that summer back in 1957. How like Hannah Ackerbloom young Caroline appeared in feature. The child ran toward Wolfgang and he grabbed her in his arms, lifting her up into the air.

"Uncle Wolfy, how about an ice cream!" Caroline said.

"An ice cream it is my princess," Wolfgang said, glad it was all over, the shoot, 1957.

He bowed toward Caroline like her king, knowing he was bowing to the generation of Ackerblooms who would take up the thread and sew sections onto this history, of which he would never speak.

Intermezzo

The Holy Ghost Wide Awake
Somewhere Over
France

(...Come inside this shrine: In the 16th Century in the South of France Mary Magdalene was the Patron Saint of Fashion Ornament. She was full of my wings flapping. Hers was the realm of illusion and change, what we are capable of, and I invisible to the world, moving images from one person to another, this is how I carry the narrative, Holy Grail. Like the silt of sleep, I make my deposits...)

V

Winter/Spring Catalogue
1999

Pure white, granular and heavy, finally there was real snow. Standing in three inches of his blessed snow, Wolfgang took a picture of a perfectly restored 1950 Harley amidst the gentle, forbearing whiteness. Behind the motorcycle stood a red barn with a weathervane atop its peak.

The sound of the motorcycle as it passed by cars on the highway in summer was the sound of a zipper unzipping. The scent of the motorcycle was the tar hot smell of summer at an old-fashioned pumping station somewhere in California, where a man and a woman sat in a red convertible about to take off, leaving their wife and husband behind. They were somewhere near the fault line everyone knows about. Yet all Wolfgang and his virile nose could smell was the tin coldness of the winter air. He felt cleansed by it, and liked the juxtaposition of the motorcycle to the snow. He knew winter to be the encapsulation of all impermanence, and relished that. But he could not hold anyone's dreams. The dreams which circled his world could only land momentarily before they subdivided and moved out again into the world at large.

When Wolfgang saw the bike for the first time, he knew it was pure. He admired the craftsmanship of it, its speed, how it would feel between his legs.

Mindy liked how it shined, it's glossy lacquer and chrome, the fact that it was valuable.

Helene wanted to feel her arms around the driver, a large, tall man.

Tim appreciated its power, its call for a leather jacket.

At least one of them thought, what a time to be alive. And it was that thought that woke up the white-haired copywriter in New York City, who when he sat at breakfast, would pick up his Mont Blanc fountain pen and write *Remember When...* on the edge of a piece of paper from his leather notebook diary in an old-fashioned cursive his father had taught him.

But soon the motorcycle in the snow would just be a photograph on page 135, splendid and alluring. After the shoot, Tim would have already slapped Wolfgang on the back, his touch confusing him. Mindy would have kissed Helene good-bye.

And when the woman near Westport, Connecticut got her mail, and looked at the photograph in the catalogue, she would have her own idea of who found love in the shadows of the hayloft inside the warm red barn behind the motorcycle. She would know by her own displacement in this world, where the dropped clothing led to, though she was both shortsighted and well educated. Yet, she eternally wanted more; more clothing, more life, more love. She wanted to be a pilgrim to the mystery of the catalogue's images as they helped to compose what was. Though she did not exactly perceive the process by which these images would lead her to buy the boots, she would, nonetheless, buy the motorcycle boots because, in effect, they were more than motorcycle boots. She would stare at the photograph of Helene in a Victorian lace wedding gown cropped at the knee wearing the motorcycle boots in the snow.

In the end it was Helene, who remembered a childhood dream she had of a dreaming, white-haired copywriter. It was Helene who knew who would ride off, come spring, into the open roads and with whom.

Intermezzo

The Holy Ghost
Flies Over New York
12.45 GMT

(…And so the copywriter must daily work in the air-conditioned abyss of his office where he could scribe what the wail of the world's dreaming said to him. His desk an altar. The hard, hard-cold wood of it so smooth, so absolutely solid, tactile, full of that incomprehensibly beautiful reality. How he loved to sit there, looking into the rocky terrain of self, mining for clues, for inner atmospherics, sinking deeply into the dream of Helene, to the secret place which expressed greatest need, to the place where *buy, buy, buy* something was the remedy to seal the need…)

VI

The White Haired Copywriter

Steven Howard had wanted to be a novelist and a poet, but he couldn't stand being alone so much of the time. Eventually, he came to the conclusion that it was not romantic to be alone with one's self until the solitude became a flower, a core bloom. Gregarious in the extreme, He needed to be around people; he needed them like a young child needs its mother. Once he thought he could possibly be a writer, back when his trust fund had still not been substantially depleted by a love of luxury coupled with a sheer foolishness about investments. Steven had thought he could write novels at the library in his free time. In this way, he believed, he could be like a painter sketching the people around him. But all morning long young mothers would be herding their small children into the library to read them books despite their protestations. He could not have imagined how many events there were for young children at the library! When he had been a child the main thing available to him at the library had been a giant *SShhhhh!* Now there was weekly entertainment for children. Folk songs were especially distracting to Stephen. He could hear the music coming through a vent from a room in the downstairs part of the library. He could hear the dissatisfied children being carried out of the folk-singing room screaming; he sympathized with their feelings. He could hear mothers calling out after the toddlers running ahead through the library. Even the adults did not speak quietly. It was indeed a different library culture than the one he had grown up with.

Once, when the noise was too deafening to concentrate on his writing, he had read an interview with Hugh Grant that inspired him. In the article, he found out that the actor Hugh Grant had once tried to write a novel at the library, but wasn't very successful at it either. This gave Stephen the idea that he would base the main character loosely on the real life character of Hugh Grant. He began to follow Grant's life in the papers and women's magazines as closely as he could stand in order to cull the media for rich details. Like Hugh Grant, Stephen's protagonist Jeremy Witt was a young, handsome English actor who had gotten busted for soliciting the services of hooker in California at the height of his career. Like Hugh Grant, Stephen's protagonist Jeremy tried to write novels (albeit unsuccessfully) in the library. However, Jeremy went to a shrink after the hooker arrest, and was trying to "deal" with the fact that his father had not allowed him to study poetry at university. Jeremy's father was a renowned novelist, and could not deal with competition from his children. In Stephen's novel, it drove Jeremy's father crazy that Jeremy was a successful actor. But when the hooker debacle ensued, Jeremy found his father happy and willing to help.

However, soon Hugh Grant stopped getting into trouble and wasn't in the news as much, and Stephen started to realize that he could neither write at home, nor could he write in libraries, on the bus, or at coffee shops anymore. He read over his manuscript and thought about how similar his father was to Jeremy Witt's father. Trustfundless, out of work, and with a very bad manuscript, Stephen Howard realized that his own father might now be willing to help him, and that he could no longer find satisfaction by living through Hugh Grant or Jeremy Witt. Within two months of deciding that he would give up writing and that the nut does not fall very far from the tree, Stephen's hair went from prematurely salt and pepper to prematurely very white. He realized that like his own father, perhaps his abilities might be better suited for business.

Still, for awhile after giving up the novel, Steven thought about Hugh Grant. He thought about writing a screenplay for *Lucky Jim* (his favorite novel), where Hugh Grant would be the lead as Jim. Then he realized the only thing that soothed his soul was Entertainment Tonight, a show he had been watching to get details about Hugh Grant. Soon he began to understand that it was creative promotion he found interesting, from an actor to a packet of cookies. So he moved to New York, enlisted his Father's help, and started a career in advertising.

One thing the Hugh Grant novel had taught him was that

he loved reading glossy magazines and watching TV, and he quickly discovered during his tenure at Ogilvy & Mather that he loved writing copy. He liked blending words he might use for some creative endeavor with the subtle nuances of selling. With a morbid fascination for cool, he relished the idea of bringing what was once counterculture into the mainstream (something he thought Hugh Grant did well with all his talk of Philip Larkin in *People* magazine) through advertising.

He loved finding clues as to what people were dreaming about. When he thought honestly about himself he was glad he had given up fiction writing. He had tired of reading Derrida and Faulkner and Melville, and was very glad to kick back at night and read *People* magazine. He was tired of living like a slob when everyone else he knew was getting rich, rich, rich. Not only that, but Stephen realized he had a penchant, a true gift, for knowing what would be cool to the average American. He wore baseball caps before everyone wore them like a disease. He had a goatee early on. Secretly, he began to dislike all novelists, and had advised his friend (he had met him through his Father) and client Senator Tom Snelling of Connecticut to support cutting off funding to the NEA, since no one he had ever known and liked received a grant.

Steven Howard was a closet Republican. To his friends he feigned Democrat. He had grown to really like the money he was making from the advertising and public relations business, and was resenting parting with a large amount of it in taxes. Not only that, but when he was a working writer and attended writers' conferences, he couldn't believe how politically correct everyone was, it immediately made him want to take the reverse stand on every issue because it had felt so repressive to him.

Once he had given up on being a writer, his father was ready to speak to him again. Things got easier. His friends from the steambath, the seventy year old twins, Irving and Max, had helped him to piece his life together and make nice with his father and find himself a wife. Slowly, Stephen's father began tentaively to let Stephen into his inner circle where the men wore their alumni ties of orange and black to three-ring affairs where the likes of Senator Tom Snelling would appear. Tom Snelling had been Mac Howard's college roommate at Princeton. Stephen tried to play the dutiful son to his father, on Max and Irving's urging, as a way out of the hole he had buried himself in through a gambling addiction and a black-belt-beer-degree and ridiculous, romantic notions of being a writer. Most upsetting to his father had been all the money Stephen had lost in his most disastrous investment to date, a company called DreamTech Engineering, a tech start-up that was trying to produce the technology to record people's dreams on VHS as they had them. But, the company was mismanaged by an old hippie who had attended Harvard in the late sixties, and had, perhaps, done too much LSD in his life around Cambridge.

On Max and Irving's suggestion, Stephen stopped writing and kissed up to his father. On a visit home for his father's seventieth birthday, He admitted something to his father that his father had wanted to hear since Stephen's mother had told him she was pregnant with Stephen and he told her that the pregnancy was not a good idea.

"Father, you've been right all along," Stephen had said on their way to the soiree at Sleepy Hollow Country Club.

"I've been a fool with money and I'm going to stop wasting my life away.

Just to prove it, I've bought this book, and I am going to read it this very night after the party."

"What is it son? I can't see what you are holding up for Christ's Sake, I'm driving," Mac Howard said from behind the wheel of his brand new, e-series Mercedes that his new wife had bought him for his birthday, with his own money.

On Mac Howard's last birthday his son had given him a used book about Peru, a place he couldn't care a whit about. Stephen had noticed his father had put the book in the guest room with the new Mrs. Howard's stacks of old *Country Living* and *Weight Watchers* magazines and unfinished sewing projects that usually contained the image of a cat within them.

Stephen looked across the car at his father's face, his nose had gotten bigger with rosacea. The light turned red, and Mac

Howard looked over at his son. Stephen tried to "be positive" and smiled at the old man, holding up the book his father considered the bible of civilized culture.

"Now there's a proper book for you son," Mac said.

"I'm glad you are finally coming around to the fact that we all have a place in society and we need to learn how to fit ourselves into it, not the other way around," his father continued.

"*How to Win Friends and Influence People* is almost as important as the constitution itself," he added, laughing a hard, old man's belly laugh, as he put the car into first gear and took off fast to pass the old dinged-up hatchback next to him.

In many ways, he was a man one could take pity on, a sensitive person could see the gapping hole in his soul in just the same way a scientist could see a hole in the ozone layer over Antarctica. Yes, Steven Howard's soul was like a large section of sky with a piece blown out of it, and this is where the inspiration for his copywriting flew in. He, himself, denied this hole in his soul, although his wife frequently pointed it out. He thought people like his wife were expert at skewing information to come up with results that could prove whatever they wanted to prove. This kept their world vision intact. But this was what Steven Howard loved about her, as well as what he hated about her. Beautiful, so beautiful was his wife, he agreed with her on most things just so he could stay with her. He was in his own way a megalomaniac, the usual advertising genius-monster. And he did love her, but not as purely as he loved the woman he had been dreaming about for months. Helene of the catalogue pages. Yes, Helene.

How he wanted to know her. But he told no one. In his mind, Helene was always walking up the beach (up the coast, a little way out... the simple things...) That was what he had written in the special vacation edition of the catalogue, and lovely Helene on an old brass bed, headboard peeling white paint, in a screened-in porch looking out to the ocean, and an old globe next to the bed representing a world that no longer existed. And Steven wanted desperately to live in that world that no longer existed; to be with Helene within the borders of that country that no longer was, to slide beneath the thin sheets of history as if each page were a spiritual bed linen. That's what he longed for, longed to fill in with the Helene (at least how he thought of her) that he met in his dreams at night after he has turned away from loving his wife's body. Each night he met her, deep in the shadow of sleep, her form reflecting light, all nights were days when he dreamt of her, his life a little way out, up the coast...that was where he would find Helene at night, on the beach looking out toward the ocean where ships once carried the New World's explorers. That's where she'd sit inside the temple of his dream, through the sand (it seemed like snow) toward the center of the dream. Sleeping next to him, secure in the dream of reality, Steven's wife knew the blankness of the gap life leaves, the sheer stark strangeness of years. One day the past evaporated (it seemed) without a sound, and when one remembered it, it was still the same, old and heavy and unchangeable as a grandfather's dusty, leather valise.

In Steven Howard's dreams years grew like moss upon the boulders on the beach. The moss grew like eternity. Helene sat upon a boulder on the beach looking out toward the Atlantic, deep in the thick air of Steven Howard's dream. The waking life was like a fog until the dream receded back toward the belly of the sea. The light of the lighthouse receded as well, shining off in the distance until the distance itself became another realm, another place to which Steven may or may not return depending upon the grace of his sleep. His sleep was the muse's visit and it hovered and shaped, elusive as time. Helene either appeared in Steven's dream, or she did not. Like eternity, she was not at Steven's beck and call. But when the shadow of Helene was made bright by Steven's dreaming (really by what controlled his dreaming) it seemed, briefly, that all time stopped. But his wife would not understand. His wife sleeping heavily beside him, so much of the human realm, not lit by the parentage of those strange earthly angels, bringing a thick nostalgia for some other sphere. And Helene's image, her green eyes and long light brown hair, her strong angular face was so full of strength and eternal youth that she haunted Steven with her beauty. So different,

Steven thought, than his wife's beauty, earth-made, by hours of blonding at the mercy of her hairdresser. Her hair an homage to a plethora of TV announcers she admired. A blonde-bobbed hair-do that came out of a history of hair-dos.

Sometimes when he looked at his wife at the beauty parlor, his eyes diverted momentarily from *The New York Times*, he thought he would like to write a history of hair. His sweet wife, who he feared would never understand the creative aspects of the sleep-life. Her sleeping life, Steven thought, was as if she were living on the moon, on some foreign terrain, without water, without beach, without tree, without meaningful image—mostly barren, with a single view of the desolate landscape of the moon life, turning and turning around the earth, effecting the tides of the ocean... *A little way up the coast...* Steven couldn't get away from it. And the sand was as heavy as snow, and the waking life as heavy as sand, grainy as film, as cracked as egg tempera. Someday, he half expected the canvas to crack and some other scene blossom forth. He was always surprised by the reliability of reality, how it was so consistent and startling. The suddenness and slowness of things was a force that he both feared and admired in the great narrative. He was overcome by the ferocity of it all , and within that drive, how simply beautiful things could be. How kingly a privilege, he thought, to walk with bare feet on the grass. And the shade of trees—how brilliant in its function and process. The way the pine tree stood in winter against the white— resting shelves of snow not made for the ground. That nature surpassed his expectations was a constant delight to Steven. Oh, sweet reality, he thought, that allowed such sleep-dreaming. And though his waking life was full and pleasant enough, he knew sleep to be a sustenance, heaven-made, a vessel where all image lay, *a little way up the coast.*

And his wife squarely and heavily beside him in their thick burgundy-purple bed linens. The linens with fringe and tassels around the pillows, the velvet piping, how tactile and smooth and sweet. How he loved the familiarity of his wife, as if she were part of the bed itself. He loved that he could always return to her, as if returning to a city one had loved as a child.

He returned to the topography of her. The scent and sense of her. To her he returned as if he himself were one of the poet Fernando Pessoa's persona-creations. He sailed back to her as if from a long sea voyage full of opium and the East's seed. His dream life full of the scent of jasmine rice in burlap bags. His dream life a white Chinese peony blooming, thrusting itself out of its orb. He had all the dread and excitement of the long voyage and a vague feeling of elation tinged with that persistent, door-knocking dread. An exacting thought that nothing, simply nothing was enough, that he might well be a stranger wherever he went, and though both worlds, the sleeping and the waking, were good, they may never be perfect enough. There was a vague and horrible melancholy in the world that he knew he shut. That vessel. That kiss. That click.

And when a silence would creep upon him as night did duly upon day—he'd glance out his window onto the perfectly solid buildings of New York. How rectangular the windows! How finite the detail! So much imagination expressed, made mundane by the pure act of living. What a grace, he thought, what perfectly crazy simplicity. That was what he himself was after in his copywriting. A crazy simplicity. Not brutish, but perhaps a bit fickle. He liked sentence fragments, thought them to be evocative of the mind's process.

And the days writing copy and dreaming and making love to his wife were always moving so quickly out to sea, up and out, over the coast. And the light always returning itself to the light. The light that Steven felt, a longing in his chest cavity, steady as a heartbeat. He loved the economy of all light, how it sat so centrally in his chest, yet could fill (if it wanted) a whole entranceway, or continent. The continents of this world always in their strange, silent shifting, such as his own longing. His own longing, he thought, cast out into the world like light refracting. When he sat there and wrote yet another caption: "Sun-ripened days…" to him it meant that all pigment was heavy with the longing of this light. He wanted to convey that all was at a pinnacle in the summer's light, and the verdancy and plushness of life near that coastline at sunrise, that softness and fleeting, was the feeling of the dream of Helene. He wanted the words of his copy to capture how things unfolded as the page turned toward the sequined white silk evening dress. A thin sheaf of words was what he needed to describe this eventuated longing where in last night's dream he traversed the great sand— as heavy as Siberian snow –pushing a wheelbarrow filled with his waking life. He had tried to go toward the place where his longing met the precise point where it was met by a force equal to it. *A little way up the coast.*

Intermezzo

The Holy Ghost
2.35 a.m. GMT
The Waldorf Astoria Lobby

(…No one appears as they are to He. This lobby is filled with the strange, strangulating tar of regret. My natural casting would be to put me in charge of all mystery, but really that's not exactly right. And I'm not all mystery either. Really, I'm more like a muse. Think of me as His muse. That might be an appealing way for you to think of me. Oh, how I like hotel lobbies—all the coming and going, how nothing really happens or changes much. I like to be the fleeting feeling of a shift in narrative, here, in the cool noise of midtown Manhattan, everyone dazzled by themselves or who they hope to be or who they'll never become, the air here dense with thought like a fog one navigates through, gliding endlessly. I am the chance encounter. I am the meeting. I am the parting. And the beauty of all lovers dreamt of but never seen, culled from my pages. I am that mystery. And there's a God who won't become flesh, yet it is He, who fleshless, makes all longing stir…)

VII

Dear Reader
Westport, Connecticut

And a woman in Westport plans her husband's life.

"Yes, dear," Kyra Snelling said again to her husband, the Senator, on the other end of the phone, as she leafed through the latest catalogue, Helene in a short, white sheath of a sequined evening gown, page 44. He was in Washington, again.

"Yes, dear, I'll make sure," she said.

In their life together, she was in charge of attention to detail and the fund-raisers for her husband's various political objectives. She was planning a cocktail party fund-raiser for his latest cause, the breeding of the so-called Numbers 19 red heifer without spot or blemish. Once an advertising industry executive, now a U.S. Senator, Tom Snelling was trying to bridge a gap between two constituencies, conservative Christians and religious Jews.

As head of the agriculture committee the opportunity to help breed a cow that was needed to fulfill scripture for both Jews and Christians seemed a worthy cause to him, even though many advised him such a cow could cause great unrest in the Middle East. It was a Numbers 19 red cow that was needed to begin building the temple back on it's ancient site in Jerusalem, which according to Jewish doctrine was a commandment that would lead to the coming of the long awaited Jewish messiah. Christians believed it would be the beginning of the end time and the Second Coming. Senator Snelling had taken a personal interest in the Oklahoma rancher's request for financial help to develop such a breed of Angus that could withstand the heat of the desert.

Long ago, Kyra had tried not to have well developed opinions about her husband's causes and projects. She just waited to see what his Chief of Staff advised as to what the appropriate political stance ultimately was. It wasn't that she didn't have a mind of her own, it was just that she was a smart politician, American style. It was all a game to her, and she liked planning fund-raisers.

117

Kyra had married Tom right out of school. When they were twenty-eight, he bought his first Mercedes. She stood there in her mother's driveway crying for joy, because that was the kind of young man she had always wanted, and because that was the kind of woman she was. That car had signaled to her in a very specific material way the kind of life she was embarking upon, and it was exactly what she wanted. He was handsome and young, before all the country club smiling had given him permanent and deep wrinkles in his cheeks and forehead.

"Yes, dear, I'll make sure it's all settled," she said again. His next political promotion (perhaps a Vice Presidential nomination?) was riding on small things like this. *Yes, dear* was her wifely refrain, her bird-song.

"No, I won't forget," she said into the telephone, as she gazed out the kitchen window toward the ocean.

"I love you too, dear," she said with a remarkable dignity, the kind that was learned from a well-heeled grandmother. Then she hung up the receiver, and began to feel an acute case of Thursday morning gloom rising in her heart. Her big heart. She was known around the Connecticut ladies luncheons as big hearted, which meant she was not completely an imbecile in taste and manner (a little too outwardly materialistic, but then again who wasn't?), and that her husband was a Catholic who had risen through the sales track rather than by having an MBA, not to mention he laughed a little too loudly.

People in some circles thought his interest in the Numbers 19 cattle a strange interest. It was, well, too apocalyptic to be chic in their circles, though it had some appeal to the New York art crowd that usually were big supporters of her husband. Senator Snelling, the chairman of the Senate Agriculture committee was working closely with an Oklahoman cattle rancher who was working on trying to breed the right color cow, one that was in accordance with scripture. It was proving to be a daunting task. Kyra couldn't believe her husband was using up his favors on the appropriation and agriculture committees to help fund this debacle, as she called it. But she understood as an East Coast elitist, her husband, if he were to someday run for a national office, had to appeal to the great, holy center of Americana.

For all her vanity and blonde hair dye, Kyra Snelling was a firm believer in science. She thought scripture was mostly bunk, a boring old story. She had heard it all before. She believed in the holy American religion of the Self, although she had not thought it through too deeply. She just knew that was where she stood when speaking with a large group, such as the Daughters of the American Revolution.

Mostly, many of these kinds of grand dames looked down on the fact that Kyra wore white before Memorial Day (even though *Vogue* didn't seem to care anymore), but still it made her big-hearted. She did not think herself big hearted, and was surprised when her friend Louise told her people thought she was. On the perimeter of her life she could feel her greed for things— material and immaterial. It was a vague recognition that she had about herself on those mornings upon which she bemoaned the previous evening's martinis. She supposed some might call her a Range Rover Republican (she had heard the term on a talk show, though she was really a very conservative Democrat but what did it matter these days), she did not resent it.

She was filled with ideas for decorating and gardening, some might call her taste "country cute" and others could never reconcile in their minds her poor taste with her large bank account. She had once positively ruined a colonial farmhouse and farm that she had bought as a retreat in Upstate New York. She had ripped out period cupboards and put vinyl siding over the clapboard and hung a sign that read "Milk 5 Cents" in the kitchen which was once the kitchen to a working dairy farm that she had put out of business by buying the place. She had built a tennis court smack dab in the middle of a scenic, sweeping pasture. She had brought suburban Connecticut country cute to the country.

But she did love these mornings (despite her tender gloom rising) looking out at her herb garden and the view of the ocean, which she had tried to paint in watercolor unsuccessfully a number of times. Looking away from her view, she looked again at the new catalogue. She saw the light of Mindy's Westchester, she recognized it in the layout, she'd grown up there, too. She could feel the wincing pain of Wolfgang's kamikaze third eye extracting everything from the scene.

Kyra thought Tim looked like her husband when they first met. He was wearing white bucks and blue jeans and a white T-shirt, too. She had seen him in the five and dime with his first love. They were getting their picture taken in the photo booth and they were laughing. She had seen the bright white bucks from under the curtain of the photo booth, and listened to them laugh. She distinctly remembered thinking to herself that no one but her father wore bucks. She distinctly remembered thinking: Whose feet are those? When he came out of the photo booth with his old girl, Kyra recalled how he looked straight at her and it seemed like the whole five and dime receded back into the void it came from, before anything had been built there. The two of them standing on the field of it, circled by that blinding light. She wanted that light back, but to have it back with all the knowledge she had gained since. She wanted to go back, to be anonymous to her life, to be less than big-hearted. She liked the white bucks on the cover of the catalogue. She liked the bucks on Tim because they reminded her of a time when she was not big-hearted, but a girl who could win over a perfectly happy young man with a single glance in a five and dime store, and that the glance could be so deliberate and purposeful, that it was already planned by something greater than herself before she had even arrived to buy a pack of cigarettes and some barrettes. That her life's course could be decided in a glance made her believe in the power of longing.

And that's what she saw in the J. Crew Catalogue, longing set out on the grand table of life. It was a language she could understand. Her desire was never satiated, but seemed to grow with each picture or view she looked at. Still, her husband's hands over the velvet of her skin could be satisfying. The silk and cashmere of her closet was a gauze for her own skin. Her house. Her view of the beach. Her car. Her children. Her fulfillment. And still desire spoke. And still desire and longing loud at the very edges of her soul, encroaching. The flat of her gym worn stomach felt empty. Her hipbones ached. Her hands always poised to crack open the slit of the canvas of life and grab still more. And it was this that made her human, made her understandable to herself. And after all the pleated skirt in the catalogue was cute with the cashmere sweater set, as was the little black suit with the peter pan collar. Ocean blue. City charcoal. Bohemian brown. Manhattan black.

She decided to order the black suit because she could wear it into the city to meet Suzanne at the Frick. And the pearls she would wear with it, like the model in the catalogue, would remind her of an innocence she still believed she possessed. The pearls had been Tom's mother, which Tom had given Kyra last Christmas. She circled the outfit in the catalogue, the exact outfit she would buy was the one Mindy was wearing, walking down the administration building steps. She bought the outfit because she was thinking of beginnings. She was reminded of that innocence she thought she might still possess. As she circled the outfit with her red marker her gloom descended momentarily, spilling out into the ocean as it hit the shore by her house in Westport, Connecticut.

VIII

Back to School Issue, Autumn
1999

Under the tent on her green canvas director's chair, Helene felt the vague nausea of dream hitting her in the center of her gut. She hoped there was no eternity as palpable as this feeling of dread. In the fragment and rubble of the day sorting itself out, Helene knew it was too much to hope that eternity would not be tactile and throbbing. She believed eternity was the undertow of the ocean.

"I wouldn't know about eternity, dear," Mary said to Helene. "I try not to think of such things. Gets the mind all tangled."

"Silly me. I don't know what's wrong with me today. Of course you don't think of eternity. No sensible person should," Helene said.

"Absolutely right, sweetie. That's the way to talk. Now turn your head a bit more toward me," Mary said.

"How's that?" Helene asked.

"Perfect, sweetie. Now chin up a bit," Mary instructed.

Mary, the make-up artist thought Helene had it too good, and that was her problem. Helene thought the make-up artist was great with color, but saw things too much in black and white. Not the ambiguous black and white of an Avedon photograph, but the black and white of stupidity. Helene felt uncomfortable with the woman, she didn't understand why Mary disliked her so much. Something to do with envy.

Sitting there Helene felt slightly changed, as if the dream (she knew someone was dreaming of her again!) had punctured the invisible film around her.

"Such a strange sky today," she said to Mary.

"What do you mean?" Mary said, as she applied a thin golden powder over Helene's high cheekbones.

"Doesn't the sky look too heavy?" Helene said, wishing she hadn't said anything at all, that Mary didn't understand anything she told her.

"Yes, it looks like rain," Mary said.

Helene realized it was useless to discuss the matter of the weight of someone's dream life upon her waking, the sheer film it left over everything; and, the heavy, sweet feeling it was leaving in her heart. It was the feeling of eternal twilight rising inside her that only the ocean could adequately soothe. The depth of the great Atlantic by her house on Long Island. She wanted to walk on the beach, meditate until everything seemed to slip back into the perfection of quiet ordinary, dreamlessness. No, Mary the make-up artist would never understand the way in which the atmospherics absorbed into everything. Mary wouldn't understand the sunlight if it didn't have to do with the way it played upon the made-up face, the shadow and light of it. The great technician of nothing, that's what Mary was, thought Helene, as she watched her own face in the mirror as it became even more photogenic under the dust of the make-up brush.

"If you don't mind me saying so Helene, I think you think too much," Mary said as she applied the final coat of lipstick onto Helene's lips, so she couldn't speak. She was applying an apricot colored glaze. When Wolfgang saw Helene on the set she thought her lips looked like an angel's lips blowing spiritus into scene. Lips that would pucker toward the guys on page 42 of the summer catalogue, doing handstands on the beach with a caption that said, "just a glance." Into those glances, Helene's kiss would land. She'd bend slightly at the waist, and then put her hand three inches from her lips and pucker to the boys in seersucker trunks. Helene did not know if she was blowing them each a kiss or sending out one, great collective kiss. Once published, the photo seemed to say the latter was right. But the copywriter looked at Helene's picture, marvelously lanky Helene, and believed she was blowing a kiss to the sea itself.

"And Just a Glance" it was for Helene as she looked out toward the imaginary sea, the place she found most solace. And in that glance all the fragmentation of things and the quickness with which they vanish. Yet, also just a glance over at three guys doing handstands on another set, young men on a fishing trip in seersucker with sweaters draped around their shoulders. Any one of them might do for a lover. Someone whose life Helene could lie up against and feel its cool-smoothness next to her own life. To be near a man's skin, letting the adhesion (of her life against the anonymity of his) peel away the film of the dream that lived around her.

So unlike the adhesion and weight of lipstick and powder that Mary applied to her face. Yet, she knew this life, this particular one. She had been leading it for some time, and it was wholly necessary, even if her brother-in-law (a non-practicing Muslim and an academic) thought hers was a highly indecent way to live, for woman or man, that these images she posed for were simply made to create a desire for things, a desire that would help make manifest the eventual destruction of the soul. She disagreed. There was beauty in the fluidity of the fabric (so like the fluidity of days), or the perfect detail of a pearl button in the shape of a butterfly. It was a fact (she had learned during her Junior year abroad in France) that during the Middle Ages Mary Magdalene had been the Patron Saint of Seamstresses, of shoe buckles, buttons and various fashionable ornaments. It was a fact Helene loved, she made it part of her own gospel. She told it to her brother-in-law, who wasn't particularly convinced by Christianity or Helene's work.

"All done," Mary said, putting her hands on Helene's shoulders.

"What are you doing this week-end?" Mary added, in a way that let Helene know she was doing nothing, and that Helene should feel guilty somehow.

"I'm going to Connecticut with my sister and brother-in-law. One of my sister's clients is having a party." Helene said, thinking to herself how funny it was to call her sister's clients, clients, and to say it out loud and seriously.

But serious it was, a lot of very serious people consulted Helene's sister, politicians, bankers, movie stars, executive's wives, sports trainers, and academics.

"What does your sister do? Mary asked.

Helene thought Mary was very nosy, and didn't like her short black hair, flawless unpainted face, and neon colored clothes.

"She's a lawyer," Helene lied; her sister Katherine was the astrologer to the elite, a dream interpreter and stargazer with an MSW from Hunter College. Stoned too often, Katherine had flunked out of Choate Rosemary earlier in her career, though Helene felt it to be a great relief, as it took her parents macro, wide-angle lens off her and put it solely on her troubled sister. It had been maddening to her parents, once hippies who had lived on a commune, that her sister could always predict the outcome of things, they had wanted to tell Katherine she was ruining her life—flunking out of Choate Rosemary! A City College! Marrying an Arab who didn't have money! But, as she herself predicted, her life went very well, as she had many "small and large blessings," that was the way she put it. Katherine was now doing very well financially (a high six figure salary), even Helene's parents had to admit they may have been wrong, and that the girl really did have some talents, if not always in forecasting and fortune-telling, then in marketing and in sales.

"Connecticut?" Mary said to Helene.

"Yes, Westport," Helene said.

"Sounds boring to me," Mary continued with the kind of envy that Helene felt only someone who had come from such a background could have.

"I suppose," Helene said, glancing over to see Wolfgang approaching with his camera still in hand.

"Have you seen Neil?" Wolfgang asked.

Wolfgang had worked up quite a sweat, and was perspiring heavily through the weave of his bright yellow golf shirt.

"Now do we look as though we've seen Neil?" Mary said in a way that Helene found rude, and thought Mary was merely trying to be edgy or cool but it wasn't coming off well. She hoped, above all, that Mary did not have the hots for Wolfgang, because that would be too horrible to even contemplate.

Wolfgang looked bewildered, as if he were a lost child unsure of his next move. He walked over to get himself some water. He looked as if he could cry at any moment.

"Next shoot sets up in three minutes," a voice said coming

from around the corner of the tent. The voice was unmistakably Neil's boyish trill.

"All done," Mary announced, as she patted Helene's face one more time. Her face was like a lost relic; smooth and timeless. And then a perfect burgundy red ribbon was tied in Helene's ponytail.

With only seconds left (she was going to be late), Helene headed toward wardrobe, and behind the curtain let her bathrobe drop. Willa, another assistant, helped fit her into the clothing, a blue and black plaid kilt, short up to the knee, some argyle knee-socks (cashmere), and yet another version of a sweater set, this one silk. Helene liked it best, she thought, as Willa pulled and pushed at her until she was the vision of someone's shopping desire.

And it was always desire that moved Wolfgang, who worked over by the set. He held his Leica in his hands more tightly than usual. Sweating, his hands were miserably damp. In his stomach it felt as if a large herd of miniature ibex were stampeding. Not sure at all, he thought, what was the matter. He felt a sense of impending doom, but he persevered by sticking to his work. He was completely sure of this particular set, Helene sitting on the grass in front of the old-fashioned humanities building—all stone with ivy climbing in a determined, collegiate way toward the sun. Neil had had a fishing net hung off to the side of the set (out of view), so that the light, as it fell over Helene, would be dappled. Neil thought he had a cunning for dappling. And Wolfgang as he looked through his various lenses toward the set, watched Helene walk on to the picnic blanket spread out on the grass. Looking at her skin, Wolfgang began to believe solely in the sheer density and lightness of it, how its cream soothed over any and all misfortune. It was, however, full of the imperfection of the world which made it somehow perfect. But, even still, Wolfgang thought, she's a pain in the ass, despite her holy creaminess. There was a sort of primitive trouble residing in her and around her, a sort of pacing back and forth quality. He believed if one loved Helene too deeply that there would be no turning back, one would simply be lost at sea, unable to return oneself to shore. One might be buoyed up by the salt of it all, but still be alone in a great mysterious ocean full of lost ships.

Neil was directing the movement of the fishing net. Helene was all gossamer of seafoam colored silk sweater set, which seemed to release the sea foam colored radiance of an icy sea. She was thinking about her weekend in Westport with Katherine and Habib. She loved parties, and looked forward to getting one last weekend at the beach. She remembered the last time they had all been to the beach together, and Katherine got too stoned and sat on the top of a dune reciting Rumi to Habib, who was very angry with her for being so disgracefully wasted. Helene remembered Habib's worried face, the deep lines of his olive skin, the way he kept burying his feet in the sand, then releasing them only to bury them again. Sitting on the set, she hoped for a more peaceful time at the beach, but in her mind's eye she kept seeing a large wave crashing against the dock with a grand force.

"Helene, Helene, we're going to move you over here," Neil said, helping Helene up, and then repositioning the blanket.

"The tassels were facing the wrong direction," Neil told her, smoothing down the sides of the blanket.

"Sit with both legs off to the left side, and then face Wolfgang. That's right," Neil said, touching her shoulder with the tips of his fingers.

"Yes, good. Look a little more to your right," Wolfgang said, his hands suddenly feeling less sweaty, as the shoot (or was it his life?) was falling momentarily back into place, snapping itself back into the matrix of it all. And when Helene looked slightly more to the right, Wolfgang could feel the world moving slightly on its axis. It was a sudden readjustment, and he felt it happening. Click, click. The shutter released. His heart was beating a little faster, then would drop back. He was feeling anxious again (why? He thought it was something about page twelve), and each time he took another picture it felt as if some new light was coming into his life, and some old light was exiting through the aperture of the lens. It was at once horrible and exhilarating.

Helene turned her head back toward Wolfgang, and relaxed

into the cage of his camera, the prison and turret of his capture. Helene could feel this enclosure of the camera upon her, the adoration of it. But the adoration came at some sort of unclear price (like the unknown price in a spice bazaar in Algeria). She wanted to stare down the lens as she might try to stare down a salesman in that same bazaar.

Wolfgang kept imploring her to look more to the right, toward the south, the dappled light.

"Look right!" he said, again and again, pacing back and forth. He expected the unexpected with this shoot. He could feel it. But he knew he hadn't captured the image, he knew he hadn't yet seen what he'd come to see. All the while, his anxiety came and went like a Westport tide, the tide Helene was thinking about. Her eyes moved like the smoke of an opium pipe Wolfgang had once smoked. The nausea of it all was hitting him squarely in the center of his forehead. Then the wind picked up and changed direction, and Wolfgang knew he would drown in his life, that he was lost at sea in the presence of Helene full of 1957, full of his mother's lavender smell floating and swimming the surface of all memory. Looking through his camera was like looking through an aquarium, distorted and sea sickening. He was no longer sure it could have adoration for Helene. Mindy, he thought, she was no longer sure she loved him, and if no woman could hold his life, he was not sure what he was capable of.

Neil had put on some Jimi Hendrix, and the sun seemed crooked in the sky, and each time he pressed the shutter release Wolfgang's heart beated, so that with each image on frame, a heartbeat thumped along. In pursuit of Helene 1957, he began to realize he had been unfaithful to his life. He believed this with the depth of his memory, which surrounded him as fully as the dream-time surrounded Helene. Nothing he had done, nothing he had sought to do, escaped this fact. He danced. Left to right, forward and back. He had lost love. He believed memory wanted him dead with sadness. Memory, sharp and wanting to slice images out of the past and puncture the present with them. The paring knife of the past whittling down the edges of the present, Wolfgang's heart racing. Somehow, he must change his life, but he didn't know how or even why. The camera in front of his face, like an extra face onto the world, a buffer between Wolfgang and everything else and Helene on the picnic blanket, so distantly close. Looking at the perfect light hitting Helene's face, Wolfgang wondered how God could stand all the images, the places, times, and faces, which swarmed through all creation.

A slight wind blew over Wolfgang. The photo shoot was almost over, because he saw everything he felt expressed in one ray of light which fell from above Mindy's beloved oak tree. It was her Westchester light, which fell on Helene when Wolfgang got the shot he wanted. Taking the camera away from his face he looked over at the tree, and heard a sudden, startling crack, and he watched as the bark tore away from wood, and a huge branch came falling down, missing him by two inches. He stood looking at thebranch. It was as if some weighty division in his life had fallen and almost killed him. He was stunned more than afraid, and strangely relieved that things were beginning to happen in his life. The branch was at least five feet long and very heavy and thick.

"Oh my Gosh! Wolfgang are you all right?" Helene screamed, running from her dappled light toward Wolfgang, who stood musing on the singularity of the event in his life, his Leica in hand.

"I'm absolutely OK," he said with a strange smile, knowing that some part of his life was permanently separated from him, pre-branch falling, post-branch falling.

Helene grabbed the Leica from his hand, and swatted him on the ass.

"Sit down, Ackerbloom," she said.

Neil was running toward them with an ice pack and a folding chair.

"Oh, Wolfgang! I was so scared. It came out of nowhere, and when I saw it falling it was too late to yell. Thank goodness you're all right. Thank God it missed you. Can I get you something to drink?" Helene was nervous; she was talking too fast. To her this was not a foreboding, just an anxiety that the course of the world, like so many other things, was not in her hands. A fear that had not been so securely in her began to grow.

"Wolfgang, come on, what can I get you?" Helene said again, wanting an assignment.

Neil was holding an ice pack on Wolfgang's head, although his head was perfectly all right, but it's coolness felt good, it made Wolfgang's thoughts even more pure, more true. The chill of it opened his mind, unturned the lock of it, rid him of the grip of muddled thought.

"Very nice," he said to Neil.

Wolfgang leaned back into the folding chair, feeling like a king over his new life that was approaching him with jewels to lay at his feet, and he leaned back so deeply that the chair fell over. All he could do was laugh. Mindy was now on hand, Neil had sent for her. Ridiculous, was what she branded Wolfgang's reaction to the whole tree affair. She knelt down beside his chair, as a daughter might. Their age difference seemed more apparent than ever.

"Wolfy, you are fucking crazy! Stop laughing," she said.

Wolfgang nodded at her, but didn't really give a shit what she was saying. Some dotted line was running through his life, which now had a force that seemed to come from the sky itself.

"And so are you my dear," Wolfgang said to Mindy. He was not going to make a big deal out of this event, it was something with a before and after, and he was going to try and enjoy the after.

Helene believed it all had to do with some general force (that dream again), that life that was flowing over them. It wasn't a violent dream despite what had just happened, but a dream that was honest to fate and chance.

"We'll need to get a doctor to look at you for insurance purposes," Neil said.

"But there's absolutely nothing wrong with me," Wolfgang said.

"By the books, Wolfy," Mindy said, still kneeling beside him as he sat in the fold up chair that seemed to small for him. "He needs you to see a doctor now, so the company can't be sued for mental pain and suffering later. Bullshit like that, Wolfy," Mindy was saying to him, chewing gum and talking, and annoying Wolfgang, who didn't believe in gum chewing under any circumstances.

"How about a Vodka Martini!" Wolfgang said, looking down from his too small, canvas throne at Mindy's cleavage, which was being displayed to him very generously at that moment.

Helene's body cast a shadow over them, producing a palpable coolness, under which Wolfgang enjoyed Mindy's splendor.

"I don't have any vodka martinis," Helene said, adding "but I have some butter rum Lifesavers in my purse."

Wolfgang definitely did not want any butter rum Lifesavers. His mother had eaten them as if they were going out of style. He had no idea that they even made that flavor anymore. Butter rum Lifesaver, like it's distant cousin rum raisin ice cream, seemed something very richly out of the past. They were a grandmotherly way to indulge. Somehow the world seemed too thin, full of sharp edges, for those flavors to exist. How surprising to him that even green pistachio ice cream remained in this world, in so many places it was now white or done away with altogether, a relic of a flavor. No, he could not endure a butter rum Lifesaver on his tongue, it would catapult him straight into the back seat of his Mother's 1957 Cadillac, not a place he felt like being at just that moment, now that things seemed to be dividing themselves for him. No, a vodka martini is what would set him up right, an old fashioned drink that still had its place in this barroom harsh world. A vodka martini, Wolfgang thought, was a masculine drink, no one really liked the taste, that's why olives or onions. A vodka martini was like being tackled in football, for the love of the game. Not like the oppressive sweetness of rum flavored things. The world, it seemed to Wolfgang, was calling for the nostalgia of vodka martinis, and all the old vodka martini making crap from the 1950s.

And then suddenly, thinking about vodka martinis, he knew that the props for the early evening shoot by the river would be 1957 martini shakers and glasses.

"Just good old American martinis," he said again to Helene, the great towering shadow. Her form bright upon his eyes as Mindy's cleavage, and the large wonderful tree limb still on the ground, a testament to his new life.

"No martinis about," Neil said to Wolfgang, handing him a Valium instead, which he didn't take.

"Time's a-wasting!" Wolfgang said, "Let's get back to work."

No one moved very fast. The tree limb and all the mess it made still had to be reckoned with.

"Well, come on!" Wolfgang said, rising from the canvas chair.

He stepped onto the great tree limb and jumped over it to the other side and walked toward the stone wall in front of the humanities building and picked up the picnic blanket and called to Neil for a clean one. Neil obliged, and handed it to Helene.

"Places everyone," Wolfgang shouted, sitting on the large limb, phallic across the grass.

"Where the hell's my camera!" Wolfgang barked at Neil.

Neil ran off to get the Leica.

"Here it is, boss," Neil said, out of breath.

Wolfgang wondered if the camera was going to lie or tell the truth, now that the line had been drawn across his life. Since the tree limb had fallen he could see how the raw edge of things were beginning to expose something previously hidden to him, how things became surreal moments before they became clear. Some first line of defense against a pure vision had fallen away with the falling of the limb almost upon him. And all the truth before was now somehow vaguely a lie, and all lie vaguely a truth. He was looking through his camera at a life that seemed somehow more sacred by its strangeness, unbarred, and loosened like long hair from a comb and shaken out with a deep exhalation.

Not unlike the long movement of Helene's hair as she shook it out. Mary was kneeling by her, touching her up as if she were a painting.

Wolfgang looked at Helene and her beauty and knew his place was firmly behind the camera. He was not a very photogenic man, though large and handsome in real life. He often wondered if the camera told some truth about him that he himself could not see. Just as the camera rendered Helene even more beautiful than she appeared in reality. Her beauty transferred to film like a relief etching that hung in a white walled museum.

"All set," Mary said, nodding toward Wolfgang.

Wolfgang decided to incorporate the strangeness of the tree limb and the mess it made into the photo shoot. He called out to Neil.

"Don't call anyone in yet, let's leave it there for the shoot," Wolfgang commanded.

Jimi Hendrix was still playing in the background. The same CD had been playing over and over for some time now. Wolfgang didn't mind, he thought it helped to lift that thin layer of panic that lay on top of everything like mist. And the tree limb, that division it made, so like a dotted line between his life then and his life now. Since the limb fell the panic was slowly rising and dissipating. His heartbeat was beginning to keep a more regular time, it had stopped jittering. With the movement of his fat, long fingers, Wolfgang focused more clearly on Helene and the dream life that was following her, thickly sprouting like blue forget-me-nots in spring.

He walked slowly around Helene, click-click (the past further disappearing), click-click (the future opening through the font of dream.) The dotted line of the world separating time and memory was becoming clearer and clearer to Wolfgang. And far off, on page 42, the young men on the beach were still doing handstands in the sand, their arms as strong and eternal as the image-dream itself. To Wolfgang it seemed the world was making a decision to make itself manifest this way, through pictures of unrelenting strength. He didn't want to fight it anymore. Helene's image would be his sword lain down, his white flag. Wolfgang continued to mine for some image of Helene that would express all the lingering beauty of the past as it incubated into the present. Helene with her perfect apricot colored lips reflected against a sheen of pearls. Helene, sweet vessel that holds the mysterious enormity of dream. Wolfgang felt the line that had been drawn in his life. He felt as if he was getting back something he hadn't realized he had lost, and Helene sank deeper into the softness of whatever it was that Wolfgang was regaining.

The robin's egg blue of the sky held the dream that hovered above Helene, and the bluest part of Wolfgang's hazel eye intensified as he looked through his lens that either told the truth or some distortion of the truth. Photographing Helene, he was aware that nothing was certain within the wash and hue of color baptizing image. Helene sat wearing her pearls and sweater set and kilt on the picnic blanket inviting everyone back into the past of the nineteen fifties to some demented realm of innocence that might sell the looker what she hoped to gain. Wolfgang shot it all, and then the film wound into its Torah-like encasement.

Wolfgang knew how to get the camera to tell the narrative of the life that wanted to be lived. His camera could find the place in any scene that stirred up desire unsatiated, the place where some part of history sat stalled wanting to move forth. This was what had made him a successful commercial photographer. He could capture this process within narrative.

Wolfgang Ackerbloom felt he was now a prisoner set free by a tree limb falling, and was beginning to wonder if he should release himself from the hold of the dream, the unattainable dream he's spent so long documenting. When he looked through the lens at Helene feeding the source of the dream (*a little way up the coast*), he remembered that Mindy no longer loved him.

Since the tree limb fell before him, he knew the lavender scent of his mother's secret lesbian life would no longer suffocate him into an anxiety where he could hardly breathe. Since the tree limb fell he began to wonder about doing some of his own photography, not only commercial work. It was a passing thought, but a liberating one that came crashing down like the tree. He had once loved the small, lovely, understated image. He had loved Joseph Cornell. He had loved the purity of his own photograph of his grandmother's hair comb that he had taken with Uncle Lenny's camera. People of his age had been interested in the likes of Diane Arbus, who he thought a phony, someone taking advantage of people, that she was a photographer with a degraded curiosity. He had turned to commercial work for the money, but also to avoid the mob-ocracy of elite art school types. Wolfgang still believed in beauty, in authorship, in being an artist for the people.

"That's a wrap," he said. And he thought he meant it.

She could feel the tendrils of some surreality spreading over her since the tree limb fell. She felt the dream following her more persistently now. Helene walked to sit under the tent next to Mary. Mary thought Helene was in love with herself.

"Whenever I'm doing a shoot these days, I always feel a strong presence surrounding me, and I know it's not Wolfy," Helene said, sitting down in a chair and looking at her nails. She was trying not to be depressed about the world. Her sister Katherine believed a dream was surrounding and following Helene, something universal and having to do with the ocean.

"You have emerged from a long time under the sea, you are coming to land. You have gained an understanding," was what Katherine had told her when reading her tarot cards.

Wolfgang was eavesdropping on Helene and Mary, and thought the dream that haunted Helene was peculiarly American.

"Hey, Helene, it's the American dream," Wolfgang said, handing his equipment over to Neil.

Wolfgang believed, ever since the tree limb fell, that their lives were being used up by the dream. He was tired of the industry's clamor for nostalgia. It was too political, too Orwellian. He was beginning to see that he no longer wanted every memory, every nostalgia, to push him artistically, or otherwise. He was prepared to escape the bread and circus of it all, but he was getting very thirsty, and suddenly weak, needing to sit down once again on the flimsy green beach chair in the grass, now near a croquet set that had been set up for the next shoot.

IX

Dutifully, the Summer Catalogue

Dutifully, the summer catalogue arrived in the Westport, Connecticut mail. Kyra Snelling walked her black lab down the long driveway to her mailbox. She heard the sound of the waves hitting the shore not too far away. A perfectly regular morning. The mail, a dog walk, the impatiens around the trees, the air having a vague sweetness that had to do with the cutting of grass. But there was no loud mowing now, the lawn man had come earlier in the morning while Kyra was in bed alone. Her husband had risen at four-thirty a.m. to catch an early train into the city. Tossing, turning, tangled in sheets, she wondered how her life had become like this, a submission to a series of dishonesties. And she had always considered herself such an honest person. Honest, perhaps, but not to herself. Discovering, desperate, she felt as if she had no more strength left. She felt a nausea that emanated strictly from the brain. Life had become a grand dishonesty filled with an overbearing sweetness of material things that left her with a sickly remorse that she told no one about. Lying in bed, listening to the constant drone of the lawnmower being ridden over a perfect green carpeting of grass, she'd wanted her life to be that evenly straightforward, like perfect lines in fresh cut grass. But nothing was really straightforward, even when it seemed so on the outside. The whirring of the mower had annoyed her, but she'd hope its sound would blast her from her bad mindset, her sad nausea. She woke up depressed, but she tried not to hold hands with it, allow it to walk clearly into the field of herself. The sheets had felt soft and warm, her body wrapped in them for safekeeping. Finally, she had gotten up when she heard her cleaning lady come in to help her get ready for the huge cocktail party her husband had commanded her to throw. Now, walking for the mail, she remembered that was why the lawn man had come so early, so he could also weed her gardens. The caterers would be coming soon in their exciting looking purple truck. She'd awoken and risen so she could let this day begin, with all its weight and heft upon her life.

Her mailbox always seemed a matter of hope. The mailbox was the receptacle that might bring some annunciatory news. She reached into the long aluminum of it, only mail that reinforced the life she was already firmly living was to be found. Bills, political fundraising requests, and fashion and lawn and garden catalogues by the dozen, haunting her, imploring her. The catalogues were the only permanence in her life. They came even when she'd asked them not come.

"Bills, bills, and more bills," she said to the dog, as her mother had always said to her when she retrieved the mail. She whistled softly, and shook her head from side to side. The dog watched her anxiously from his post beside her.

Full of the weight of her dissatisfaction, she walked up the long driveway and admired the one thing she always admired, the morning itself. She liked the way the morning came over the past, which with every new morning seemed bright, back lit, brilliant. Her past was receding like a hill. Like a hill in Vermont she had often tried walking toward, but it always receded somehow in the most disorienting way. But toward her house she walked, past the well-coifed lawn of it, toward her desk work, this mail, that cocktail party her husband required her to throw.

"Good morning, Mrs. S.," her housekeeper said to her.

"Just look at all this junk mail! I must get thousands of these catalogues a year!"

"Here let me help you with those," Veronica, the housekeeper said, putting down her dishrag on the back of the sink.

"No, no thanks. I'll just get my coffee and be out of your way," she said to Veronica, the last cleaning lady in Connecticut to still do windows without being asked.

She went to her father's old roll top desk with her mail. She lay the mail down, blew at her coffee and took a sip, staring briefly at the photograph of her and her husband that sat framed on the right side of the desk. The photo had been taken the summer they were first together. She liked the photograph, a record of what seemed to her to be something that was fast disappearing between them. Having the photograph helped her to remember how she'd once felt. The photograph was the one remaining document of the tenderness she had felt. The two of them stood hand in hand on his father's farm in Vermont, she in her long wrap around skirt and French T-shirt, and him just off the old Ferguson tractor in a pair of worn blue jeans and his blue Yale T-shirt with holes in it. Her hair had been long and full then, it's original color, less blonde. Her arms seemed outspread, though she held his hand. It seemed as if she'd wanted to embrace everything that would come.

Her husband did not understand why. Out of all the professional portraits of the two of them, this picture gained such prominence in her life and on her desk. The quality of the picture was, in all honesty, not terrific. It was a grainy old Instamatic photo that had been enlarged. She felt the enlargement only added to its appeal, and that the photo spoke to her about how she had come to love her husband in the first place.

She ran her index finger around the frame, and set it back on its spot on the desk. She leaned back in her seat, put her feet on her desk, moved the mail to her lap, and began leafing through the catalogues—though she should have been busy with preparations for the party. There was no resisting. The catalogue that caught her eye was the one with a pair of men's bucks, beautifully photographed in their whiteness. They were exactly the shoes her husband used to wear. The tag line under the bucks said, "Buck Naked." She opened the thick, glossy pages of the catalogue and stopped on the page where Mindy and Tim were walking down the college steps with Caroline running ahead of them into the future beyond Wolfgang's camera. In Mindy's eyes looking backward toward Tim in his white bucks, Kyra saw herself looking at her husband back during their days at Yale; back before her hair was this blonde, back before she cried in strange joy over the first sportscar he purchased, back when she believed in the wonders of a charmed life. But now she realized her charmed life had just become routine and boring. She had landed in her life as if it were a room of comfortable white pillows. A place for infantile souls too filled with spiritual birth defects to handle a more rigorous Karma. She had gotten used to comfort and thought nothing of the discomforts of others. Her only sadness was this vague coating over her life, a dull sheen. She wanted to be as carefree and attractive as the young women in the J Crew Catalogue, though she was not completely conscious of this aspiration.

The clothes Mindy wore on page 33 came in Nautical Navy or Lake Isle of Innisfree or Pink-Peony in addition to the Pitch Black she wore. The Peter Pan collar, the classic pearl buttons reminded Kyra that she wanted everything. She wanted desperately to believe that life was her little pet, her sweet, obedient dog. Looking through the catalogue, Kyra believed she might find some deeper meaning if she could live some strange rehashing of a Holly Golightly kind of life, wearing red lipstick, drinking martinis, and slipping into an outfit like the one Mindy wore on page 33. She thought she might even be willing to risk her charmed life for a moment that felt like the one Mindy portrayed walking down the steps of the Humanities building. Kyra believed deeply in this catalogue religion. Yet, she wanted to flirt with the Fates, get out of her five hundred-dollar cashmere sweatsuit. She wanted to look back on everything the way Mindy was gazing back at Tim on page 33.

As Kyra looked back at her life, she gazed with less certainty. Her own son and daughter now off at college. Her husband still handsome, still fit. Still, though she believed in the charmed life, how it was better than anyone thought, but she wasn't sure at all why this thin film of sadness. The way her husband still always smelled of the six-ten train even when he took the car. On this day, she would tell her new spiritual advisor all about it, the woman named Katherine who channeled healing dolphins. Her neighbor Amy had told her about Katherine. Katherine had done a spiritual reading for Amy and her husband, a former ambassador to France. At first Kyra thought it would be merely an amusement, but now she thought she needed the reading like a drink.

But until Katherine arrived, there was a cocktail party to get organized. Katherine would walk over from Amy's later and

Kyra would serve her tea and sandwiches in her study with the roll top desk and the old picture of her and her husband. In the meantime, she thought she should get dressed, but thinking about her closet, a virtual room in and of itself, she felt she had nothing to wear. Looking out at her garden, she decided that her life would always increase with more and more bounty despite her sadness. Strictly on the merits of her life, she would confide every inch of herself to Katherine to see what could be done. For now, she would order the bucks for her husband, Mindy's 1950's outfit for herself, and by doing so she prayed more deeply at the altar of her life.

Lunch-time arrived carrying the smell of soup cooking from the kitchen. Kyra called out to Veronica.

"My guest and I will be having lunch in my study, could you be a dear and bring it in to us after she arrives?" Kyra said in a way that was neither too nice, nor too bossy.

Kyra watched for Katherine from her study window. Amy would instruct Katherine to walk to her house on the path the women have made from Amy's garden to the Kyra's garden. She waited anxiously to see what a spiritual-advisor woman looked like, for she has also invited her to her party that night since Katherine and her husband were staying with Amy and her husband, Dick. She hoped Katherine was not too way out, and would fit in with the other guests, sometimes Amy's tastes could be a little eccentric. Indeed, the visit with Katherine was being paid for by Amy as a birthday gift to Kyra. Kyra was not sure what to make of these new age people she read about in *Time* magazine, but she listened to Amy as a little sister listened to a bigger sister.

She could see someone walking under the wisteria that was draped over a trellis. Then she could see Katherine emerging through a stand of oriental grasses, swiftly passing the roses with a great surety of stride in a long purple skirt that met her ankles. Her straw hat was covered in dried flowers, most notably a sunflower seemed to jut out of her forehead. Kyra thought the woman looked rather pale, and had the look of a bookish girl she once knew in high school. She had thick wavy blonde hair, and probably, Kyra thought, unshaven legs. Pear-shaped was the word that came to Kyra's mind as she watched Katherine cross the freshly mown grass and toward the door. Kyra moved from the window of her study and sat on the white and red chintz sofa, and waited for Veronica to show Katherine in.

She could hear Veronica's slippers making their way to the door. She heard the cowbell on the door jingle, and then the two women coming down the hall to her study.

"You must be Katherine, so glad to meet you," Kyra said, extending her hand to her.

"What a beautiful spot you have here," Katherine said, shaking Kyra's thin, smooth, manicured hand. "Your garden is sheer perfection," she added.

"I've been so looking forward to meeting you, won't you please have a seat?" Kyra said to Katherine, not sure at all that she should have accepted this gift of Amy's, a reading of her life. She felt like Nancy Reagan, having this guru to her house.

"I thought we could have lunch in here. Can Veronica get you something to drink?" Kyra asked, surveying Katherine's hands, a minefield of turquoise rings.

Kyra pressed the button on the intercom for Veronica, who came back right away bearing a tray of tea and saucers, soup and small crustless sandwiches.

Over the tea and sandwiches, Katherine explained the whole procedure.

"We'll begin by monitoring your aura," she said.

"And how do you do that?" Kyra asked, a little concerned that monitoring her aura wouldn't turn her into a zombie.

"With a laying on of hands, I can both see and feel the color vibrations of your aura, and see where in your body you have power shortages. Then the dolphins will assist us with their sonar capabilities in order to heal you, " Katherine said matter of factly, drinking her tea.

Kyra was sure she had no power shortages. She had begun to wonder if Katherine had a history of drug abuse that had slowed down her ability to think rationally.

"Don't worry, I know it sounds strange, but when I move

the energy of your aura around, you will feel a shifting and an opening in your life. You'll see. I can tell just from looking at you that there are some blockages," Katherine said, dusting sandwich crumbs off her chest.

Kyra was astounded.

"I've finished your astrological chart with the information you gave me over the phone, and I've charted some things I think you'll be interested to find out," Katherine added, taking two small bells out of her purse as she stood up.

"Why don't you go ahead and lie down on the sofa now so we can get started with the reading," Katherine said.

With some trepidation Kyra crossed to the sofa with some trepidation and lay down stifly.

"Don't worry," Katherine said. "I'm not going to do anything weird. I'm just going to ring these bells over your body to let the universe know we are beginning to undertake the work of the spirit, that we mean well, and are trying to create an opening for ourselves."

Kyra tried to relax, but she felt as if an invisible spirit was choking her, that a deep and unnerving kind of spirit hovered above her.

Katherine moved her hands quickly and then more slowly over Kyra's body. She wasn't touching her directly, just her aura. Her hands were about two inches above Kyra's skin. The longer Katherine did this, the more relaxed Kyra felt. Afraid she might fall asleep, She began to think of her husband that one summer they were in Vermont together before they got married. It felt as if whiteness were running through her, not quite a dream, but a dreamlike whiteness. For some reason, she couldn't help thinking of the white bucks on the catalogue cover. The image was lodged in her brain like a bullet. Katherine's hands kept moving. Kyra thought of the white bucks again, and had a vision of her husband on their wedding day, the laces of his white bucks always going untied. Kyra got the sense that Katherine was trying to mold the invisible above her. Her fear had dropped away, and she felt as if her whole life was being kneaded like invisible bread above her. She could feel her life part of a dream that was floating in and out of the room. Katherine rang the bells around her body intermittently.

"The dolphins will be our guides today," Katherine said, clapping her hands. Kyra could hear the clink of Katherine's rings, and then a tape of the ocean began to play. Still sleepy, Kyra thought dolphins seemed like a stupid, corny idea.

"Good, I can see you are relaxing, now we'll begin the visualization. Take a deep breath through your nose and then exhale slowly through your mouth," Katherine instructed.

Kyra obliged, breathing slowly in and out, trying to forget about the cocktail party that evening. Katherine told her to start visualizing herself walking through sand toward the sea.

"See the white crests on each wave. Imagine there is a sea-temple out beyond where the waves break. Go toward that temple, there is a bridge that lets you walk above the waves if you believe in it," Katherine instructed, her hands still floating above Kyra's body, the tape still playing ocean and dolphin sounds.

Kyra imagined the beach of her childhood, the beach she still lived by. She imagined it devoid of the fishermen and the ferries, the sunbathers and the washed ashore detritus. She saw herself seeing herself. She saw her old red pail and wooden spade, a moat made around them in sand. She saw the apple she had left uneaten, it's white core collecting sand as if the apple were a magnet attracting tiny particles of steel. She saw her old beach towel with the long, long tassels on the end. As she imagined herself walking the beach she could feel gravity holding her onto the world. She could feel a small piece of tar sticking to her foot. She could hear the loud screams of children running toward the ice cream truck. Still tall and painted white, she could see the lifeguard's chair with its red and white umbrella. She could hear the loud shrill of the lifeguard's whistle piercing into her memories.

Opening her eyes, she saw Katherine's hands stationary above her head. Katherine's eyes were closed. Kyra thought the woman was in a trance, and that scared her. But it also made her want to laugh. To laugh as she had once laughed on the beach, as if she might lose her mind from joy, as if her whole self might spill from her like milk through the nose. She could not laugh now though. Katherine's hands above her face stopped her as a stop sign at an intersection stops cars.

Yes, intersection was the main feeling, lying there breathing deeply and thinking about the seaside. She was at another intersection in her life, that was it! The mere word seaside made her think of fried dough and boardwalks and whiteness. White light, white clothing, white sunblock over noses. If she laughed now it would be the distorted laugh of the house of mirrors. Now, with this barrage of memories about the beach and the sea she must try to imagine dolphins calling out to her to come, to come to the temple.

"I'm realigning your energy now, you should begin to feel more centered soon," Katherine said.

Lying there thinking about the beach was what it felt like to Kyra.

"OK, now what do you want to ask the dolphin guides?" Katherine asked her.

"I don't know what to ask a dolphin," Kyra said.

"Keep concentrating on the ocean, on the temple, on the waves," Katherine instructed her.

She imagined the temple. White light flooded from it, and she imagined the light surrounding her. She felt stupid, but she tried to imagine herself in it's white light.

"Good, I can feel you in the temple," Katherine said to her, "What do you see in the temple?" Kyra saw her deceased grandfather in a white robe reading the *New York Times*. She saw her mother as she was thirty years ago in a gingham bikini doing a crossword puzzle. She saw her old school friend Annabelle Sterns, twenty years old again, walking toward her from another part of the temple with a tray of drinks with pink umbrellas.

"I see a lot of sand," Kyra said to Katherine.

"The dolphins are helping you to get on with your life, to leave behind past lives," Katherine was saying.

"What past lives? I'm thirsty," Kyra said, suddenly feeling extremely parched. "And sand is infiltrating the temple!"

"The dolphins do not want you to see the dream for some

149

reason, they are blocking it from you. You must not be spiritually ready. I think we'd better finish for now. We need to work more on your energy fields first, realigning them. This is not out of the ordinary, after reading your natal chart this morning, I thought this might be the case," Katherine said, ringing the bells around Kyra's body again.

"Let's try some rebirthing breathing," Katherine said to Kyra.

All Kyra could think of was Lamaze breathing, which had never worked for her, she thought it a cruel joke it was just a cruel joke. Katherine was reminding her of one of the Lamaze teachers she'd had at child birthing class, one of the teachers who had given her a book called *Spiritual Midwifery*. The teacher had presented this book to Kyra when Kyra declared that she would take every possible drug to be knocked out during childbirth. To Kyra, Katherine looked exactly like one of the hairy, big bosomed women in that book talking about the value of pain and not swearing during childbirth. No, she did not want to do the breathing exercises. She wanted to finish planning her party now.

"Please, don't get up yet, we need to try the breathing," Katherine said.

Kyra was just feeling thirstier and thirstier. She had had enough.

Katherine put on a different tape, but it was still dolphin sounds.

"These dolphins will help you break down any spiritual barriers in the way of your enlightenment."

As she tried deep breathing, tried to let the dolphin's sonic sounds heal her charmed life, Kyra felt her thirst begin to rush and deepen in a way that was almost intolerable, as if she were stranded in Arizona on a dusty road at high noon. She jumped off the sofa, rushed toward the tea tray, and drank a whole cup of lukewarm tea as fast as she could while Katherine rang her bells in each corner of the room.

Intermezzo

Holy Ghost's Lament
3

Love is my only hope, my thickest grief.

X

Kyra Snelling's Cocktail Party

Everyone arrived in the twilight that hung over Senator and Kyra Snelling's white farmhouse. Cars were parked by young men in khakis, the Volvos and Audis lined the hill of the driveway. A false magnificence fell over the scene; the well-coifed lawn, the rose garden, the scent of sea air against the soft smell of men's after-shave. The women followed the men out of their cars and onto the grand patio and deck overlooking the Atlantic. Kyra had specified, black tie affair, and now she was glad. Everything, everyone looked so healthily impenetrable. She liked the neat fix of each man's cufflink, the careful walk of the high-heeled women. Safety, she believed lay in this outward display of detail. But she was still reeling with that strange, unquenchable thirst since she had visited with Katherine and her spiritual dolphins. Imagining dolphins with Katherine had merely made her thirsty. A tray of champagne went by her and she reached out with a desperation she had not yet felt in her life. She had already consumed four large bottles of Pellegrino water since Katherine had gone back to Amy's to dress for the party. A drink, she thought, might dull the desire. But it did not. And then Wolfgang walked by. She had known him for years through her involvement with the State of Connecticut Council on the Arts. On this night, he looked different. She hadn't realized he had a business connection with her husband, as well. She was going to find out how they knew one another.

"He hired me on as a freelancer once, and now I'll be photographing a spread for Vanity Fair about the Senator and his Numbers 19 Red Cattle Project," Wolfgang told her.

"Which kind of freelancer were you? Did he hire you when he was in advertising or politics?" Kyra asked.

"Is there a difference?" Wolfgang said in a flirtatious way, raising his left eyebrow at Kyra, then grabbing a piece of toast with caviar from a passing silver tray. He knew he didn't know what he was doing, or why exactly he had come to this party. He hated these kinds of parties.

"You're a funny one," Kyra said, feeling a bit like her mother, feeling a little lightheaded from the champagne.

"I was the one who did the photos for his '88 senatorial campaign," Wolfgang said, talking with his mouth full. But it did not turn Kyra off. She felt a little strange, and had a silly and startling passing thought that she might kiss Wolfgang on the beach.

"Oh, yes, now I remember. That was a marvelous campaign, everyone said so," Kyra said, reaching for another champagne.

That was the first year her husband had been in the Senate.

"What a wonderful year of parties followed that," Kyra said. She was one of the Washington wives who loved, even thrived on fund-raisers.

"Those little parties are like spinach to me, they make me strong! Some people think that kind of life means you don't have a life, but I'm more alive then!" Kyra said, appearing a little drunk, spilling some of her drink on Wolfgang's shoes. Wolfgang looked at Kyra quizzically.

Out of the corner of his eye he saw that Mindy had arrived with Tim. She had never said anything to Wolfgang outright about Tim. Now it seemed over in a public way, with Tim escorting her to the party. Wolfgang felt misery about to descend, but Steven Howard walked by, a little drunk as well.

Steven Howard looked as though he thought he would never have what he wanted. Though it seemed he did have it all, it did nothing for him in the same way some expensive suits do nothing for their hunched over owners. A bit drunkenly, he thought about the beach, about his new campaign, *A Little Way Up the Coast*. He had heard that Helene was to be at this party, and he was trying to remain sober enough in case he might have a chance to see her and talk to her. But the night was perfect for drinking, he thought. The stars and moon were out and the whole of Long Island sound seemed as glossy as his best campaign. The night hung thickly about him, as tactile as his own desire. He surveyed the deck and did not see Helene. But he bumped literally into Wolfgang.

"Wolfgang, my man!" Steven Howard reached out his hand with the sureness and grace of those who have read Seven Habits of Highly Effective People.

As they shook hands, Wolfgang felt the gin sweat oozing from Steven Howard's hand into his own.

"Good to see you!" Steven said. "What's it been about one year?"

"Since that hunting trip!" Wolfgang said. The two men laughed.

They had been on an agency male bonding trip together to shoot bear in Alaska the summer before. Wolfgang remembered how scared Steven had been at first, and also remembered being a little alarmed with the amount of gin he'd consumed before loading his rifle. Wolfgang had taken riflery in college and had a healthy respect for weapons; they scared him.

Steven looked at Kyra and took her hand and kissed it, "Mrs. Snelling, I presume?"

"Yes, and you must be…?" Kyra said.

"Howard. Steven Howard," Steven said.

"Well you two, now that we've all met, let's take a walk on the beach!" Kyra said suddenly, as though it was one of those rare moments when she got the clarity of a really good idea like serving lobster bisque and a clam bake at her husband's last fund-raiser. She liked the gnawing nostalgia of a theme. Tonight's theme, she thought, on such a beautiful night should be the beach. "I do so like to see men in evening attire barefooted on the beach with their trouser bottoms rolled-up," she said, winking at Wolfgang.

Wolfgang thought it was going to be a long evening, now that he also had a drunk Steven Howard to baby-sit. Once Steven got hold of you at a party there was no getting rid of him. Wolfgang decided early to go with the flow, to maintain a Zen like stance.

"Terrific idea," Steven concurred. "You're the toast of the Great State of Connecticut, my dear."

And with that he raised his glass of blue Bombay gin toward the clear night sky. He was having a premonition of Helene. Helene sitting on the beach waiting for them.

Wolfgang and Kyra linked arms. Kyra's husband was talking

to Amy and Richard about what it was like to have a baby in France these days. Amy's daughter was busy trying to get pregnant in Paris with her writer husband, and living off Amy and Richard to a large extent. Kyra's husband found anything French fascinating. He also found religious issues fascinating, as well as fundamentalists of all kinds, though he himself was not one. The cocktail party was a fund-raiser to help Israeli Jews and an Oklahoma cattle breeder produce the biblical red cattle that would help to signal the return of the temple to Jerusalem, and hearken the coming of the messiah.

"Come," Kyra said, and she took Steven Howard with her other arm and lead the two men down the steps of the great patio-deck, across the lawn and down the path through the garden to the sea.

Kyra in the middle like Dorothy, all searching for their own private Oz to make the evening more interesting. All Kyra could ever think of was her father's imploring, if you can't get it done by midnight you aren't ever going to get it done. It was only nine-thirty, and she wasn't sure what that piece of fatherly advice had meant nor did she care. She was of a certain age now.

"Ready!" Kyra exclaimed, grabbing the two men by the arms once again. The dull hum of the cocktail party could be heard against the regular heartbeat of the waves. Occasionally, Kyra could hear the deep, meaty laugh of her husband echoing through his kingdom—of which she was sure she was the princess. Wolfgang and Steven were her courtiers. Still filled with her dolphin-initiated thirst, she had brought with her a bottle of bubbly for her and her companions. They strolled and avoided jellyfish. The tide splashed against the edges of her simple, long, white Calvin Klein evening dress. Wolfgang's rented tux was getting a bit wet, but it felt good. Steven remained oblivious to the sensuality of the ocean, so thick was he with the mission to find his Helene tonight. Headline: *A Little Way Up the Coast.* He was on the edge of falling into a hopeless drunkenness, but for now that edge was a place where all was possible, where all the magic of his own surrealism was true. How he loved French champagne.

"The night they invented champagne," he began to sing.

Wolfgang thought, *oh no*, please.

Kyra shrieked a sorority girl shriek she was famous for in Georgetown during the time when the Senate was in session, and she spent time in the Georgetown townhouse.

Wolfgang was beginning to think he should go back up to the great deck and patio and smoke a cigar with the Senator. Wolfgang was about to unhitch his arm from a singing Kyra, but he saw something moving on a dune in the distance. He could hear a distinct, low humming sound. Both Kyra and Stephen seemed oblivious.

"Can you hear that noise," he asked.

"What noise?" Steven Howard asked, as he tipped his head to the side and pretended to listen in earnest.

"That low hum," Wolfgang replied.

"Here little dolphin, dolphin, dolphin," Kyra called to the ocean, laughing. She was telling Steven about her 'little rendezvous with Katherine, Sorceress to the ex-French ambassador's wife.'

Steven was letting her know he could be persuaded to believe in such things, though she clearly was not sure what she believed herself.

"*Sshh!*" Wolfgang commanded. "Do you hear that?"

"Certainly, Wolfgang my dear man, that is called the ocean," Kyra said.

Steven laughed the way dopes laughed. He was very tenuously on the line between drunkenness and oblivion. He farted and didn't even realize.

"Sulfur!" Kyra said, inhospitably, then laughed again, drawing from the Moet bottle as it stuck to her lipsticked lips. She had released her grip on Wolfgang's noticed this, and ran recklessly ahead of Wolfgang, toward the dune as if he were going to steal base and slide into it on his stomach. As he ran in a zigzag manner, his bow tie came undone and fell into the sand. Wolfgang was aggravated, Steven was usurping his one adventure of the evening—and after an especially aggravating week where he had seen his sweet, young Mindy had fallen for Tim. The hum got louder as Wolfgang approached. Steven was bent over the long grass, kicking a path to where the hum emanated from.

161

Kyra stared at the tide, wishing for a small, smooth piece of blue glass to wash up by her feet. She always wondered why blue glass seemed to live in the belly of the ocean.

"Mother told me to go to Radcliffe, but did I listen? No, no! A million times no!" Kyra was saying. Her drunkenness was beginning to take hold, take a turn into the morbid vault of should-haves.

Steven's feet were beginning to hurt, thrashed by the pampas grass he stomped through. Wolfgang joined him on the dune, peering through the long grass, searching. Wolfgang smelled burning, he remembered the stench, the memory of it stuck in his throat. The pampas grass reminded him of Vietnamese jungle. The salty air aggravated the wound of it.

"Here's the culprit, boys," Kyra said, and whistled loudly as if hailing a cab.

Wolfgang and Steven looked down from the dune like lost children having won at playing King of the Mountain. They stared at the naked Katherine, who was sitting, humming, in a meditative position. Kyra picked up Katherine's dress and put it gently on her.

"Why am I so thirsty?" Kyra demanded.

Steven was still staring at Katherine's body, not pretending to have any social decency or decorum. Katherine reminded him of her sister, Helene, and finding a naked Katherine on the beach made Steven now believe anything might be possible. Wolfgang sighed.

"You know Wolfgang, the French say a sigh is a desire for something you do not have," Kyra blurted out.

"What are you doing out here? What are you doing buck naked?" Steven asked, as he sat down next to Katherine, who maintained her composure. She kept quiet. The quiet was beginning to lull Steven, who took out a crooked cigarette from his squashed pack. He thought smoking might revive him. He could see two figures approaching from the left. It was Helene and Katherine's husband Habib.

"It's inexplicable! I say!" Steven said, trying to align a match and the cigarette he was trying to light. It was as if one of his drunken eyes was making one figure in the distance fuzzy, and the other figure fuzzy as well but with a kind of moonlike nimbus.

"Do you see that, my dear. It's simply incredible," he said to Kyra, motioning her over to sit on his other side. "Why that's my sister Helene and my husband Habib," Katherine said.

"Now, Miss Katherine, you still haven't answered my pesky little question. Shall I say it again?" Kyra looked at Steven, raised her eyebrows and frowned, trying not to laugh so as the precious champagne would not come out of her nose.

"Why am I so damned thirsty—and not to mention where are the dolphins? Will they be greeting us this evening? Or are we awaiting the sacred cow to moo right toward us, walking on water like Jesus Christ himself!" Kyra said, and then began to laugh. She didn't realize she was being rude, vaguely she had the feeling that she was entertaining Steven, who with a bent cigarette in his mouth looked toward the luminous person in the distance.

"Bored, lonely with the ache of a few drinks, Wolfgang walked down toward Helene and Habib. "What the hell is he doing?" Steven Howard muttered, taking a long drag from his cigarette and then coughing.

"Who cares!" Kyra said. "Oops! I didn't mean that! I'm a bit tipsy," she added, suddenly realizing her station, a Senator's wife, drunk with a bunch of fund-raisers for a sacred cow that was supposed to bring on the messiah's return to Jerusalem. "You guys are far out," Kyra added, she was drunk, there was really nothing she could do to save face, and she realized that.

Momentarily Steven forgot about Wolfgang walking down the beach toward Helene and looked over at Kyra and smiled. He was thinking maybe he could sleep with her. He was thinking he was too drunk to drive home. He was thinking about some copy he wanted to write, something about the moon's nimbus and the beach and the moment's sure death and uncertain resurrection and how it had to do with poodle skirts. The drinking was beginning to make him feel philosophical, especially since Kyra had brought up that cow. Being a religious man in the most superstitious of ways, and remembering that Kyra's husband was involved in helping to finance the breeding of the Numbers 19 cattle that would signal it was time for Jews to rebuild the temple, made Kyra appealing to him. He believed

Kyra's efforts at fundraising for this cause of the Senator's made her part of biblical history. He wanted in on that. He wanted to be biblical, in the best PR sense.

He momentarily lost sight of the figure on the beach, but then he saw Ackerbloom standing near Helene, staring at her. Habib had walked on and now sat in front of his wife, Katherine.

The sand felt good against Wolfgang's feet as he stood by the ocean, by Helene. He liked the wet, heaviness clinging between his toes. He liked the chill of the evening air ruffling up underneath his white tuxedo shirt, which was now untucked and unbuttoned at the top, his tie bunched up in his pocket. He wasn't sure what he should say to Helene. He realized he wanted to take a picture of her looking like this, bearing a light, a celestial weight. He wanted to capture the starkness of her face. He wanted the fear he felt inside to move out of his center with the fluidity and grace. He could feel himself being freed of his mother's control. He had no camera with him, his protection, his guide, his way back out of fear. He wanted to reach his arm out and let his hand gently touch Helene's shoulder. He did not want to listen to the flapping beach gull's wings of fear. The tree had fallen in his life, it meant no more fear. He was deciding to be whoever he was before that fear adhered to him like an image on film. He was going to try and get what he really wanted.

Standing by her, he could see how she was as vulnerable as any winged thing. He saw the ocean move in toward them, the tide getting higher and higher. It seemed to Wolfgang that the world was infused into Helene's beauty, a beauty which would not hold him captive. Looking at her he felt the feminine prison of his mother was lifting from around him. "Looking good," Wolfgang said. He knew what Helene was doing was called Tai Chi, but he didn't know the first things about it. His ex, the stripper had been briefly into yoga until she got stuck in the plow position with her legs thrown over her head. Wolfgang had pulled her out of it, and she walked slumped over for three weeks. He had never heard the end of it. Watching Helene he hoped her foot would not get stuck in that position where she holds her foot in her hand before sticking her whole leg out in the air.

"Does wonders for the hips and the lungs," Helene said, putting her foot in the cup of her left hand and turning her leg out. "Have you ever done Tai Chi? I'm doing a variation on it," she asked him.

"No, no I haven't," Wolfgang answered, deciding not to tell her about the yoga incident.

Helene unlatched herself, and turned toward Wolfgang, gently grabbing hold of his arms and moving them through the air.

"Feel that, really feel that," she said to Wolfgang.

She was teaching him.

No one noticed when Helene kissed Wolfgang on the lips, lips with a silty residue, not of salt, but a substance of sleep, slightly soporific. She kissed him more deeply and felt a yearning within her. The silt was the dream's deposit, she was sure of it.

Their kiss was interrupted by the sound of Kyra's voice.

"Wolfgang, can you help me get Steven up to the house, darling? Habib and Katherine had left, Wolfgang could see them walking down the beach back toward Kyra's house. Every few minutes Steven would shout out slurred words beginning with 'Did you know' either trying to ask a question or tell a joke. It was annoying.

Wolfgang had had enough. He wanted Helene to himself.

"Let's get them out of here," Helene whispered.

Wolfgang and Helene helped Kyra get Steven to his feet. They all walked back up through Kyra's garden, up toward the lights that hung about the great deck like a promise, like a future. Wolfgang couldn't get there fast enough.

Helene slowly followed Wolfgang, suddenly seeing in him a strength she had never noticed before. A strength that was concentrating on the pointillist lights strewn on trees. A strength made of mere molecules of light. Surprised, beach weary, wide-awake for the world, she followed toward the Senator's brightly-lit house.

Intermezzo

2.41 a.m. GMT, Bermuda Triangle
Lament 4

(Love. This is my only hope.)

XI

The Day After
The Snelling's Cocktail Party

Steven Howard awoke with what he thought was a terminal hangover in a room he was not familiar with. He was on top of a pink and white chintz coverlet perspiring heavily, sun streamed through the window and onto the five o'clock shadow of his stubbled, red face. Confused, parched, he was not at all sure how he had wound up in this perfumed room that smelled like a department store he used to frequent as a boy with his grandmother. The room made him want to vomit. Sickness welled up into his throat and then choked back, he sat up a bit. Leaning against the laced and ruffled pillows, he was sweating too much to think properly, and then he realized he was still wearing his tuxedo jacket. He took it off, it reeked of a fetid champagne and vodka perspiration. The white of his tuxedo shirt tried to soothed him; he pushed up the sleeves and swung his legs to the side of the bed. He could smell coffee brewing. He farted. He ran his hands through his hair, looking in the mirror he tried to pat down strands that were sticking up.

The day was coming into view as he began to recall where he was, the Senator's house. The Senator's wife, Kyra, the one with the legs. He had walked on the beach with her last night, he thought. What had happened? He vaguely remembered a naked woman, then after that it was all fuzzy. He remembered being barefoot. He remembered that Wolfgang Ackerbloom was there, too. Nervously, he rubbed his teeth with his index finger, he hoped he wouldn't bump into the Senator, that he had already gone out for a run, or whatever it was Senator's did in the morning. He wanted to keep his account with the Senator as a freelance writer, even though the Senator seemed strange these days, obsessed with the recreation of a biblical cow. The Senator had urged him to write a speech on this very topic, for another fund-raiser he was attending to help underwrite the research and development that would produce the red cow. However, the

Senator's Chief of Staff had canceled the speech, and the Senator instead quietly attended, cracking jokes all evening with a table of ranchers who hoped to get a cut of the pie that would finance the whole biblical proceedings. The Senator saw this scenario as wildly interesting, and also as a way to get both the Jewish and Fundamentalist Christian votes.

Steven Howard felt sure he had slept with someone but he was not sure who, though he could occasionally smell wafts of Channel #19 drifting from his hair. He would have to figure out who wore that scent, then perhaps the night would come more into focus. He remembered the blonde, thick hair in his hands, the thin taut body beneath him. A knock on his door startled him as he stood there beginning to remember his love making scented with Chanel #19. He opened the door slowly as if something startling might pop out from behind it. A cup of coffee pushed it's way through first, then a hand on his chest pushing him back into the the flowery, department store–like bedroom. In came Kyra with teeth so white, Steven thought he might go blind. His questions were being answered as she came closer to him.

"Good morning," Kyra said with a voice that made him both weak and revolted.

"Kyra, I was just about to come looking for you," he lied.

"I came to see if you were ready for our outing?" she said, pushing his hair behind his ear in a way that annoyed Steven. He was beginning to think about his wife, and wondered if he had called home.

"What time is it?" he asked her. She looked at her Rolex.

"Time for the outing, sweetie!" she squealed.

He didn't have the heart to ask what outing this was. It appeared to be a beautiful Saturday morning, rays of sunshine flashing through the window onto Steven sweating back. Kyra bit his ear.

"Here's a shirt and some shorts if you like," Kyra said. She had brought in a some of Tom Snelling's clothes and put them on the table by the door. Under no circumstances did Steven want to wear the Senator's summer duds and accompany Kyra to whatever outing it was. Although with her there in front of him he remembered walking down the beach with her and Wolfgang.

"Darling, we're going to the beach! Come on, drink up!" she held the coffee out to him again. On the table sat the Senator's Izod shirt and LL Bean khaki shorts. Had she really expected him to wear those clothes with his dress shoes? He began tabulating in his head the ways this affair would help and hinder him.

"Where's you husband?" he said.

"Off to the club for a full day of charity golf, then flying to Oklahoma to visit with that cattle breeder, " Kyra said.

For her part Kyra realized she slept with Steven because she was drunk. She'd loved her husband, but now she had landed drunk in the middle of a strange adventure. Katherine's dolphins had made her thirstier than hell, and this was the outcome. She hadn't felt such emotions since her parents had left her at summer sleep-away camp for the first time. She felt like the young woman she had been, in a madras dress riding in her father's sea blue Cadillac, smoking her first cigarette with her girlfriends as they drove toward the drive-in. She leaned toward Steven and kissed him squarely on the lips. They tasted of booze. He needed a toothbrush. Kyra didn't care, she kissed him, walking him backwards, toward the bed.

Steven came up for air as she landed on top of him. Her mouth over his made him feel as though he were suffocating, as if she were a receptacle for every image, every idea he had in his life. Her blonde hair in his face made him feel as if he might never write another word of copy, as if she were sucking all out of him. He felt that making love to Kyra once more would keep him from ever writing good catalogue copy again. Looking at her, his heart began to palpitate in an uncomfortable way. Desperately he tried to think only of the beach, not of Kyra's warm body up close against his. When he thought of the beach Helene came to his mind. He thought about all he had built, his apartment back in Manhattan, his summerhouse on Montauk. Resolutely, he pulled his stubbled face away from Kyra's and simply said, "No." Then he lied and told her.

"I can't, your husband's a client. I couldn't look him in the face."

"That wasn't a problem last night," Kyra said, trying to kiss him again.

He pushed her gently away, and began to get to his feet. "I need you," Kyra said, feeling thirsty again. In some crazy way Steven was like the source of a spring to Kyra, it was as if lying on top of him she had found water by diving for it with the rod of her body. Every inch of his body against hers felt like a definitive text, like a concordance that would help her better understand herself. He was referential to her, she understood that, but would never be able to talk about it cou in an intelligent way. Instead, she got up too and went into the bathroom to quietly cry and leave Steven to show himself out.

Steven did what he always did in matters of love, he began to feel guilty. He pounded on the bathroom door. "Come on, Kyra, that doesn't mean we can't be friends," he said through the bathroom door, he could hear water running out of the sink that Kyra had turned on. Still he could hear the sounds of her wailing and sniffling.

"Friends? What do you mean, friends?" Kyra said. "Come on out, Kyra, this is silly. Let's be adult about this," he said, pleading with the wood of the door. He felt as if he were leaning against the cool grate of a confessional. The door made him feel as if he could say anything.

"Come out, you're a beautiful woman. I'm sorry, I don't know what I'm saying," he said through the invisible grate of it all. The untruths he whispered led him closer to oblivion than the booze had the previous night. "Do you really mean that?" Kyra said. He could hear her turning on the water again.

"Of course I mean that," Steven said, adjusting and scratching his balls, trying to return them to a comfortable place. Kyra came out of the bathroom, and he touched her hand in a way that made her feel as if the outing were still on, and though he felt it a kamikaze action in the most creative of suicidal ways, he took her hand in his and asked her, "so where is this outing anyway?"

Kyra laughed, "Last night Wolfgang Ackerbloom saw me

coming out of the bedroom where we'd left you in earlier and invited me to the photo shoot, the one you're writing copy for. It's at the beach just up from here."

An elixir of terror and joy ran through Steven heart. Generally he tried to stay away from photo shoots as they broke down the dream of the dream he was trying to create. He didn't like to see the segmentation of it all, how Wolfgang constructed his stories. Artistically speaking, he wanted to remain pure in some sense, to come to the material with his own sensibilities about what the dream should say to the viewer. And now he was with a viewer, he could tell by Kyra's pedal pushers and pink button down shirt right out of the spring catalogue. He had written the copy for the spread they were part of, Breaking the Bonds of Time. And now he wasn't even sure why he was going to go with her to this photo shoot, though he had to admit he felt guilty for the sex they'd had. He knew that a Senator's wife was not to be fool around with, so he decided that he should go, 'only as a friend, you understand.'

Steven had never been this nice to a one-night stand in his entire life. Something was suddenly quickening within him. Really he had wanted to be an adult his whole life, but he knew not how. He had a horrible inkling that this was what might be happening to him. Still, he was thinking of Helene, mostly. Thinking of Helene softened him. The senator was off golfing, and then going to help the breeders of the sacred, apocalyptic cow, the least he could do would be to comfort Kyra back into the submission that lured her into the dream life of catalogues and flowery bedrooms. Steven would lure her back there to leave her and then try and get on with his own life, and he hoped this little escapade would not interfere with his copy writing abilities.

"I'll have a wonderful time if I'm with you," Steven said, agreeing to spend the day with Kyra.

As he said this he thought of how he might see Helene at the beach, and his heart quickened. Kyra mistakenly saw this emotion as something for her. With great verve, Kyra grabbed Steven by the hand and dragged him down the stairs toward the kitchen where she planned to seduce him over some more coffee, before depositing him into her white Volvo station wagon for the ride down to Wolfgang Ackerbloom's section of dream beach. Steven gripped her hand with the fear that the non-swimmer has for the ocean itself, and followed her into her kitchen where he could smell the coffee.

Kyra poured him a cup and handed it to him.

"Drink it, you'll feel better," she said.

"Thanks," Steven said, looking out the kitchen picture window, past the trellised garden and toward the ocean. He could feel the salt clinging to the lining of his lungs. He could feel Kyra trying to look into him, and he imagined a fisherman's net, like the one his father used to use in Maine. He imagined the net shielding him from whatever wanted to enter his dream life, the life that sustained him. It was then that he realized he had not dreamt last night, or if he did he did not remember. The blonde of Kyra's hair blinded him in the sunlight of the kitchen. He was trying to trap himself in the net of his imagination where his dream life would be safe. He watched Kyra pack a beach bag and put her dark Audrey Hepburn sunglasses on, the ones from page 57 of the spring catalogue. "Let's shake a leg lazy bones," she said to him, lifting up her sunglasses.

Steven wasn't sure how he could ever write his way back into the dream out of this disaster. While Kyra went into the downstairs bathroom to fix her make-up he snuck back upstairs to change into the Senator's beach clothes, and to call his wife from his cell phone.

For her part, Kyra felt clearer than ever, as if she's suddenly changed from wonderful to incredible. She felt as if she were living the kind of life she had glimpsed in Chanel advertisements and JCREW catalogues. What she was living was really plain adultery. The plainness of her adultery was so plain that she mistook it for something elaborate and as ornate as her imagination projecting itself onto the world like a movie projector producing sleek images. It was all coming together for her, but her thirst continued. She planned on putting her hand on Steven's thigh in the car, and then smiling at him under the open sunroof.

178

Intermezzo

The Holy Ghost Dreams
of Tending the Roses in
Stratford-Upon-Avon, England

(Simultaneously in time. The Holy Ghost sometimes dreams in Shakespeare's sonnets.)

"When most I wink, then do my eyes best see,
For all the day they view things unrespected;
But when I sleep, in dream they look on thee,
And, darkly bright, are bright in dark directed.
Then thou, whose shadow shadows doth make bright,
How would thy shadow's form form happy show
To the clear day with thy much clearer light,
When to unseeing eyes thy shade shines so!
How would, I say, mine eyes be blessed made
By looking on thee in thy living day,
When in dead night thy fair imperfect shade
Through heavy sleep on sightless eyes doth stay!
All days are nights to see till I see thee,
And nights bright days when dreams do show thee me."

XII

The Cover, a Beacon, Summer
1999

Sweating, stifled and hot, Wolfgang took his red bandanna from his back pocket and tied it around his head to block perspiration from dripping into his eyes and stinging him mid-photo. He'd been waiting three hours for the light to be just right, for the talent to emerge from costume. His neck hurt from talking into his cell phone for too long. He smelled something in the sea breeze. What was it?

The swoop of the Connecticut coastline was like a mantra to him, the waves rolling toward the beach continually reclaimed his attention when it wandered off into a memory. Vietnam. A helicopter landing on the beach, the heat, the tortured run of a small girl toward the chopper as it lifted up into the air filled with the dead who needed identifying, and a live Wolfgang and a live pilot. Sometimes another memory would hammer on the door to his consciousness: 1960, his mother and father standing on the lake in the U. P., the chill of the air and the chill of the strain between them. Then it was 1957, and in his memory he saw his mother kissing her lesbian lover. Each memory preserved in the film emulsion that was his mind. He reminded himself: this is Connecticut. The waves sang to him like healing sirens not to go back, back to where memory resided. The waves asked him to create photographs purely out of this moment, full of the Atlantic meeting the shore. The calming sound of the waves reminded him of the tree limb falling, that crack of the branch. He remembered how he had decided that the fallen branch would be the demarcation between then and now, before and after, fear and no-fear drawn across his life. With his mind, like a wall of fire, he held back the fear. Today, he would pursue an image that would bring him glory. If he could get a picture of the dream in all its gossamer wonder, it would be his last stand in fashion photography. He would have completed his mission for the catalogue.

For Wolfgang that image would be of Helene running down the beach, out of history, out the straining dream narrative that he had become tired of since the tree limb fell. He wanted to capture this running from the dream as the dream approached. If he could get this shot, he would feel as if he had done what he'd wanted to do. Then he would freelance, pursue his own creative work, something void of dream history. He wasn't sure what that would be yet. Perhaps he would just hold his camera out of car windows as the car went zooming down the road and try to capture that exhilaration. But for now, he knew that he must focus on the task at hand, get the image he had come to receive.

The shoot began. Helene had said nothing to Mindy about the cocktail party, how she and Wolfgang made love in the Senator's study on top of his bearskin rug, from a bear he had shot on a hunting trip with the one time Secretary of the Interior, James Watt. She told Mindy none of this, but knew it was now both separate and apart from the dream someone had been having of her. Now she knew Wolfgang was part of the dream, she had tasted it on his lips as sure as sugar. Gluttonous, Helene felt now, she understood where the dream resided and she wanted to catch it as a child tries to catch a bird by its tail.

Mindy thought she could never get enough of Tim, he was like rain that falls, that sound she loved against the windows in spring. That sound that brought the earth back from its penance of frost, that force which makes the crocus. Her desire for him was so like that. Mindy saw him wink at her when it first began, and she stared right back at him, she didn't care. She no longer wanted to play the coquette; she wanted to admit to everything that the world required her to admit to. She wanted to admit something to Tim. This was the last time she would look at Wolfgang in this way, with her eyes piercing him and his camera. She no longer wanted to be his image. She ceased wanting to be seen merely as shape and color and the mover who makes the desire into sales through Wolfgang's crazy alchemy of lens.

And then Helene was running beside her, harder and faster. Green gingham bikini order number T5353. A horse's hooves, Helene could hear them in the pounding of her own chest. The sound swelled up in her ears like ocean water. All she wanted to do was to run down the beach as far as she could for as long as she could endure.

In Helene's feet kicking up sand, Wolfgang could see the young girl he had photographed, lost from her mother, the smoke of their village hanging in the backdrop of the air, which seemed unbreathable, was unbreathable. The beauty of Helene was the positive, the fear and screaming of the lost girl the negative. It was as if at this instance, these two moments held Wolfgang in the dichotomy that was his life, his containment. History was leaking into him and through him.

Losing his breath trying to keep up with Helene, the erosion of the present against the past began once again to open Wolfgang's mind to his Vietnam photographs. Those nights he had slept hardly at all, boozed up and dreaming a strange dream of a young American woman running down the beach in a bikini, who kept looking back at him, strange red cattle behind her in the distance. He'd had this dream night after fetid night. It was of the gold ore inside a dark, dark earth; the yolk of the resurrecting egg. It had haunted him. It had helped to drive him from photojournalism like some kind of crazy curse or drug problem. And now he was witnessing that dream image, trying to capture it for his paycheck, for the cover that would proclaim the tag line, a little way up the coast. It was déjà vu and yet it wasn't déjà vu, but it was stylized. It was purely dream, pure as a newly fallen mango, so fresh one still heard the snapping of the fruit from the limb. That was where Helene was headed, up the coast of Connecticut toward the vanishing point. In her running she was the unobtainable, the one risen from the sea, pure Botticelli. Wolfgang knew he was the only man who could ever hold her in her entirety, that he would be forever linked to her. Still the visions of this Vietnam dream he'd had held onto him, followed him along the beach.

His Vietnam time dream was so clear again, watching Helene, the smell of her still on him, as pure as the sweat of their lovemaking had been. It was pointless, almost, he thought, to try and get the shot of Helene. He was out of breath. But she had stopped. She was standing by the water, her big toe in the water, looking out to sea. He had seen her, photographed her many times before, but he had never seen her like this, dreamlike, of his dream and of this dream. What luck, he thought. Quickly, Wolfgang put his lens back up to his right eye so as not to lose whatever dream was circling Helene, making her more beautiful through his lens. Overcome, he began to feel a mood overcome him as one feels weather coming in from the sea. With his Leica in hand, he took shot after shot, transfixed by the definite, strange beauty that flew over like an M. C. Escher bird pulling in the future out of the distorted past. But Wolfgang was having trouble keeping up with Helene, she'd started running again.

Neil handed Wolfgang a water bottle. Wolfgang grabbed the water and drank it, letting it flow through his body. He climbed in next to Neil and they drove through the sand toward Helene who was approaching a dune. It was pointless to keep trying to take her photo for the cover; she was out of the set. But Wolfgang kept keeping on, he would not surrender this image, as he had surrendered others, putting the image of his mother and her lover away in an attic storage box, or the photo of the girl in Nam screaming down the beach running toward Wolfgang in the chopper filled with dead GIs that he left somewhere he could no longer find.

He wanted to capture this image as other men had captured countries. The negative on the film hanging in the dark room would be the liberation flag hanging defiantly and strongly. Photography had power to defy reality. He was living within earshot of the image he had dreamt of almost thirty years ago in the night jungle. The newsman he once thought he was smelled something. He was coming close. And as Helene sat on the dune looking out on the Atlantic blue longing of ocean, Wolfgang captured her as the sole inhabitant of an important dream habitat that was, for the moment, not built upon, still pure in it's inducement to desire, thick with that certain slant of light and shadow, and an acutely particular dream life.

Back along the beach under the tent that had been set up for the crew and the equipment, Kyra and Steven sat drinking Diet

Cokes. Steven saw Helene receding into the distance, Wolfgang chasing her. Looking at Kyra, a banner to every headline he'd ever written, he felt like a man lost, deposited in another dream, different from the dream he thought he was dreaming. He began to lose track of what was going on, his muse of the dollar bill was flying straight over him. Helene was heading for a vanishing point on the beach, and the sun shone through that point, enduring, mysterious. He could sense that Kyra would never leave him now, that the previous night had cemented together all that would be and there was nothing he could do about it. Seeing Helene close up, being near her, only made his dream recede. He could see that now. Being close to Helene had made his life spin out of control. He looked at Kyra and she was smiling at him. Steven Howard could now understand that the dream life had it's own course, that it had merely used him to acquire this moment. Wolfgang's image of Helene running up the beach in the gingham bikini that would be their best selling bikini ever.

Wolfgang could feel the fear in his body flying away like bats into the evening sky. With each shot of Helene he could feel the future building, he could feel something heavy but loose coming upon him like sleep. It was with this feeling that a new look appeared on Wolfgang's film. The new look promised something different but the same, a different narrative, a different present. He was capturing images of the shoreline as English ships had captured it hundreds of years earlier. Wolfgang saw he was an explorer, intimately involved, he was now both the captured and the captor.

But the horizon was still there, and though the sun was setting, it seemed to Wolfgang as if Helene ran down the beach faster than the present or the future, and that the sea air was thick with her, with dream, perfuming the moment with a rose scent that it would always hold. In the end, he got the picture of Helene sitting on the dune in the best selling gingham bikini ever, the light around her a pearly nimbus, a beacon of promise.

www.ingramcontent.com/pod-product-compliance
Lightning Source LLC
Chambersburg PA
CBHW021230020726
47498CB00008B/2785